To.

Enjoy!

Shelton Ranasinghe
12/29/2016

HEAVEN AT SETI'S DOORSTEP

By Shelton Ranasinghe

This is work of fiction. All of the characters, organizations, and events portrayed in this book are either products of the author's imagination or are used fictitiously.

Heaven at SETI's Doorstep

ISBN: 978-0-615-38292-0
Copyright © 2011, by Shelton Ranasinghe
2665 Devon Hill Road, Rocky River, Ohio 44116, USA
sr2665@gmail.com

Library of Congress Control Number: 2011912434

First Edition

Printed in United State of America

Lovingly dedicated to the kindest woman on earth my wife Dilani and to my two wonderful children Ayesha and Sajeev.

•••

Sincere thanks to my good friend Bunchy Rahuman for his wholehearted efforts to improve my book. His expert knowledge of English, clear and objective viewpoints and brotherly attitude were what I appreciated most.

Heaven at SETI's Doorstep

SETI institute seeks evidence of life in the universe outside the earth. SETI is an acronym for Search for Extra Terrestrial Intelligence. Their main activity comprises scanning of the skies for any radio signals or radio waves originating in outer space, presuming they are sent by intelligent beings living on other heavenly bodies. According to current scientific thinking, life can originate and perpetuate on any planet with a suitable environment, given a sufficiently long period of time to evolve and stabilize. Once life emerges, evolutionary processes will eventually lead to development of a life form equipped with a special 'thinking organ' with the ability to develop advanced technologies, similar to the processes that took place on the earth. Based on this fundamental idea, extraterrestrial life forms could be expected to exist and be detected and communicated with. To this end it would be necessary to employ a systematic full spectrum, daily scan of space and listen in on the widest possible spectrum of radio waves to mitigate possible scanning misses. However though the universe had been scanned over the past four decades and millions of dollars had been spent on this research institute; no detections had been made thus far by it. SETI Institute is funded entirely by donations from individuals and grants from private foundations. This shows the immense support for and enthusiasm of the public for such research.

Seemingly as if in reward for the dedication of the staff; on 7th August 2011, SETI Institute was hit by a strange radio signal from outer space. Wow! This was the rare moment they had anxiously awaited over, decades. Within a few minutes, the whole facility exploded in excitement as the news passed back and forth. It gave a sudden boost of adrenaline to everyone. The emotions and reactions of the thrilled staff were wide and varied. Some were speechless or dazed, many were shocked, yet others felt that the instruments in use needed to be checked. Almost everyone could not believe it had really happened.

While it was no doubt a time for everybody to cope with their emotions, the devoted scientists and technicians were not unduly distracted from the task of following up on the extraterrestrial signal. All sensing equipment was seamlessly fine-tuned to pin point and lock on to the source and to record the input with the highest possible clarity and detail. Of course, the greatest emphasis was on verifying if the signal had any coded information, seeking a response from us, "Humans on the earth". Unfortunately and to everyone's utter disappointment, the signal faded out sharply after, lasting for nearly fifteen minutes, and totally disappeared without any prior indication. Being conscious of the enormous significance of this event, the staff tried vainly to re-detect and establish contact with the signal over the next several hours. Everybody understood the immeasurable good fortune of being able to detect the signal and the 'once in a lifetime' rarity of this event. If there had been a message in the signal, the inability to reply would have been a great tragedy. Opportunities for communicating with alien beings from any part of the universe were necessarily a rarity. It would be a great misfortune if such an encounter were not exploited. However, with time, and due to the inability to detect even the faintest of signals from the original direction, efforts at signal re-tracing were abandoned. A feeling of emptiness mixed with disappointment remained and the only consolation was the possibility to extract clues from the information that was recorded during the total period of contact with the signal.

No time was lost in initiating analysis and research on the recorded data. Teams of experts were formed to look into areas that needed specialized data evaluation capabilities. Appropriate specialists were immediately contacted to supplement the efforts of their teams. The foremost task was to confirm that this was a signal from outer space and not from any other source linked to earth. Verification of this fact was a minimum requirement for the institute, before any news could be released to the communication media. It was widely known that clandestinely operated radio equipment was in use by various parties, by-passing laws and governing regulations. The possibility that the detected signal originated from any such sources had to be conclusively eliminated by thorough checking. Considering the major repercussions of erroneous information being transmitted through the media, extreme caution had to be exercised in the release of information to the public.

After months of sustained and laborious analysis, cross checking to eliminate the possibility of other sources originating the radio signals and reviewing the opinions of many scientists; the data evaluation team was able to narrow down the source of the signal to a sizable space object that had come into the 'field of view' of the scanning instruments. This space object was a very large meteorite well known to astronomers for decades. But a radio signal had never before been detected as emanating from this meteorite. A few more weeks of exhaustive study verified that this particular space object was radio inert. This was confirmed by past observed data as well as further scientific investigation and analysis. The meteorite concerned was passing the moon at a distance of 3.5 million miles at that time the signal was detected. Considering the relative proximity of this object to the moon and the earth, the only possible explanation was that the signal was in fact a wave reflected off this object and the point of origination of the signal was an abandoned manmade radio instrument on the moon. Further analysis coupled with simulations run and re-run, checked and re-checked, confirmed beyond doubt that the signal had been transmitted from the far side of the moon. As there was no line of sight from the far side of the moon to earth and also due to the specific position of the object relative to the moon, the data evaluation team, was forced to the conclusion that the signal was a radio wave, reflected off the space object. Before a final conclusion was confirmed, further mathematical calculations were performed using the most advanced programs and computers which took into consideration the position of the moon, the earth and the distance to the meteorite; the result was even stronger evidence that the signal was transmitted from the far side of the moon. However even the most sophisticated techniques and experts combined with the best computing resources could not detect a code embedded in the entire 14.76 minute recorded data of the signal which somehow seemed to have a pattern. All experts associated with the data evaluation assignment were highly motivated and very pleased about the opportunity they had to work on the project. Most of them volunteered to provide further support to probe deeper if they were called upon to do so. Still however, SETI Institute did not wish to release news of the events at this stage and had reservations about the source of the signal. Moreover, they were concerned about adverse comments that might be made by the public and other professional researchers.

The obvious first follow up task was to check if the signal could have resulted from accidental re-activation of a manmade device landed on the moon earlier. To verify this, details of all probes that man had ever sent to the moon were perused. This was dated back to the early nineteen sixties, the time moon explorations commenced at a very minute scale. Gathering all the information was a very tedious task considering the number of countries involved and the fact that many explorations took place nearly half a century ago. SETI Institute needed help from the many countries involved in moon exploration but preferred to conduct the information gathering task in secrecy. As a result, many countries from which information was sought were suspicious and perplexed and could not understand the need for this historical information which to their thinking could not serve any purpose. Much time passed by and SETI Institute was getting desperate as the required data was not forthcoming as readily as expected.

As time passed, SETI Institute realized the importance of having the cooperation of all the countries to help them in their work. They understood they had no other alternative than to divulge the purpose of their request and to be truthful to the scientific parties in all the countries associated with their search. After this change of attitude, many sources of assistance were forthcoming to provide the necessary information. But there were also many groups who ridiculed them as a bunch of lunatics wasting public funds. Gradually, a mass of comprehensive historical technical data was acquired on operations involving placing of 'radio-live' equipment on the moon's surface.

However, even after careful sifting through all the information compiled, it was not possible to identify a single manmade object on the moon that could have generated the signal. All the evidence seemed to be pointing towards the possibility that the signal originated from the moon itself!!

Seeking Assistance from NASA ••• ••••

To determine the actual status, it was decided to seek the assistance of NASA. This was at the time NASA was concentrating on Saturn's moon Titan after the Cassini and Huygens spacecraft brought back images and information of extremely high clarity on Titan's landscape. After a top level meeting between the scientists at the two institutions, NASA agreed to help. They offered to send a special purpose orbiting satellite to the moon to verify the signal, but on condition SETI Institute would provide the funding.

Very great precautions were taken prior to releasing the news to the public. Because a message of such nature answers our psyche's very fundamental question of "are we alone in the universe?" it could have major philosophical and sociological impacts on the human population. The media had created panic situations in the past on the subject of aliens even with simple radio broadcasting that was meant purely for entertainment. However, in spite of the secrecy exercised, the news had leaked out in to the public domain through various sources. Hence, it was no more a secret. The alien signal was the hot topic dominating the TV news in many countries. Here was an opportunity to attract public support. Funds began flowing into the 'signal exploration project'. As the funds were flowing in, the project was also gaining momentum. There were varied reactions by the public as is usually the case in such instances. These reactions were openly published and discussed over the media. Some activist groups argued that money should not be wasted for projects of this nature and should be diverted for humanity enhancement projects. Some religious groups also objected to the project. There were reactions even within the NASA community as to whether they should undertake this project. However a very large percentage of the public supported the project with great enthusiasm.

In the midst of all these reactions, things moved and progressed very well. SETI Institute was very happy about the overall outcome as they were in command of the project and kept the public informed of project progress through their web site, twitters and other social media. After nine months of hard work, NASA launched a custom built satellite to orbit the moon looking for radio signals. The satellite launch was a flawless event without a single hiccup. After four days involving flight, directional and speed corrections and other maneuvering and exchange of command signals, the satellite was placed on a stable equatorial orbit of the moon.

The satellite was programmed to detect a signal when it was orbiting above the signal's transmission area. As the signal was determined to have been transmitted from the far side of the moon, detection obviously would take place when the satellite was also on the far side of the moon. When this occurred, the satellite had no communications with the earth as the moon acted as a barrier between the earth and the satellite. As such, during this orbital time the satellite was programmed to record all the information it received. The recorded information was then transmitted to the earth when the satellite was passing over the visible near side of the moon. Based on the data of the original signal, NASA had sufficient information to focus the satellite's antennae to the 'transmission area' of the original signal.

Four days after the launch, the satellite was in an orbit around the moon as planned. All instruments were tuned in to detect the signal. This was an anxious moment for the SETI Institute team as well as for the NASA team. But the anxious waiting of both parties was rewarded only with disappointment for seven consecutive days as the satellite was unable to trace any signal. The calendars were all marked for one full week of 'no result' and the teams were losing hope and adjusting themselves to lower expectation levels.

On the Eighth day, Bingo! A signal had been detected. The satellite was a success! It detected a very steady signal. According to the data transmitted to the earth, the signal was beamed from a location in the region of the crater "Daedalus". The altitude instruments in the satellite, with capability to assess distance with an accuracy of one eighth of an inch, also indicated that the signal did not originate from an object on the surface of the moon but from beneath the surface of the moon! In other words it had been generated underground in the moon! This was checked and re-checked and found to be correct. This was astounding news.

According to experts who interpreted the data, the signal generation point was at least 30ft below the surface of the moon. The exact location of the signal was established and confirmed by the GPS instruments in the satellite. The impact crater "Daedalus", was very familiar to NASA and was known as a region which had a very vide area of flat terrain. NASA scientists verified that this particular signal location was thousands of miles away from the nearest possible spot where a man-made object had ever touched down or even been deliberately crashed on the moon. As the satellite was circling the moon at a low altitude, it could be in touch with the signal only for about 27 minutes. NASA was keen on putting the satellite to a higher orbit the next day, to increase the signal capturing time. Unfortunately, disappointing everybody, the satellite started spinning during maneuvering. This could not be corrected despite all the remedial measures tried out. However, the detection of the moon based signal by the satellite was sufficient to conclude the signal's existence, precise location and the fact that it was generated from below the moon's surface. Everybody was anxious to learn more but they would have to wait - the monitoring satellite had turned into 'space junk'.

Detection of the signal from the moon was groundbreaking news to the entire world population. People reacted in many ways; each with their own theories to explain the possible sources. The media did not waste time in capturing the people's imagination and publishing the multifarious theories and explanations. These ranged from intelligent underground life colonies of the moon to alien established sophisticated radio monitoring stations. Some even said that there could be people like us living in the moon's underground. In the midst of this extraordinary discovery including the underground source of the signal, NASA backed by SETI Institute had an emergency meeting and it was decided to evaluate and re-establish NASA priorities. The Moon Signal Research Project was the unanimous top priority selection over many other projects that were in the priority ladder.

Planning committees were formed. Various brain storming sessions were conducted. Ideas were flowing with abundance to determine as to what was to be done next. A manned moon probe was an obvious long term solution, but they were well aware of the infeasibility of it in the very short or even short term. Such a mission was estimated to be at least a decade away even on an accelerated basis. As an interim measure, one of the strategies considered was to have two satellites in Luna-synchronous orbit. One satellite was to be stationed above the spot from where the moon signal originated, and the second satellite at a place such that it had direct line of sight with both the first satellite and the earth. The basic idea was to have the first satellite pick up the moon signal and transmit it to earth immediately through the second one. This arrangement would allow NASA to receive the signal continuously as well as perform more interactive experiments and testing as they wished. Both satellites had to be stationary relative to the moon such as in a Luna synchronous orbit for this to happen. This idea while having positive attributes involved some technical problems to sort out.

Just a bit of Rocket Science now, to sort out the technical issues!

NASA had to find something corresponding to geostationary orbit when placing the two satellites in orbit round the moon. In the case of the earth, finding a 'stationary' orbit is quite easy. Just use of high school math would yield the radius at which a satellite will be in equilibrium when orbiting the earth at the same angular velocity as the earth's spin. This radius works out at 32,000 miles and the term "geosynchronous orbit" is used to refer to this specific orbit. The name of science fiction writer Arthur C Clark is also given to this orbit as it was he who was the first to write about the usefulness of this orbit. Doing the same calculation for the moon, Luna synchronous orbit works out to have a radius of about 64,000 miles. You might think the radius should be much less because of the low gravity of the moon but it is not so due to the slow 28 day orbital period of the moon. Can a satellite be kept at 64,000 mile radius orbit round the moon? No. It is difficult and problematic. Unlike the case of geostationary orbit, where the gravity exerted by the relatively low mass of the moon is insignificant on satellites orbiting earth, the earth's gravitational force on corresponding satellites orbiting the moon is quite high. As the earth's gravity tends to overwhelm the gravity of the moon, establishing lunar stationary orbit involves a complicated problem. Mathematician Leonhard Euler (1703 - 1783) discovered however that there were three points on the line joining the centers of the earth and the moon, at which the combined effects of the pull from the earth and moon generate the exact required centripetal force to keep a satellite in Luna-synchronous orbit. Mathematician Louis Lagrange's later fuller investigations showed up two extra points where this fine-tuned balancing was achieved. These two points were also unique in that they allowed very stable orbits compared to the viable but somewhat unstable orbits at the first three. These five 'equilibrium' points named Lagrange points after Louis Lagrange are usually denoted L1, L2, L3, L4 and L5.

These equilibrium points are located as follows:

L1 - Lies between the earth and the moon, on the line joining their centers. This point was irrelevant to the project.

L2 – Lies 37,000 miles behind the moon on the extension of the line joining the centers of the earth & the moon.

L3 - Lies also on the same line passing through L2 and L1, but is on the opposite side of Earth from the moon. This point was also irrelevant to the project.

L4 and L5 – Lie on opposite sides of the apexes of the two equilateral triangles - one above and one below - with a common base formed by the line joining the centers of the earth and the moon. Being at apexes of the equilateral triangles, the distances from the centers of the moon and earth to these points are equal and are 238,000 miles while the lines from the earth and the moon to these points form an angle of 60 degrees with the line joining the centers of the earth and the moon.

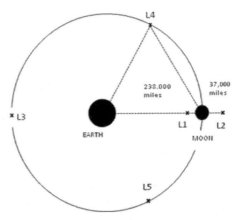

NASA found that according to the available data, Lagrange Point L2 was almost directly above the spot from where the initial moon signal originated and hence was an ideal point at which to station the first satellite to pick up the signal. The second satellite that was to be a relay unit was to be located at Lagrange Point L4 which had direct line of sight with the earth as well as the first satellite at L2.

Once again, as news of the planned missions was spreading around the world, the public expressed their great interest and enthusiasm in supporting the exploratory missions. Major companies in USA and other international corporations offered ready support. Project funding now seemed to be the least problem! This was very encouraging for SETI

Institute. Space exploration enthusiasts were very optimistic that the investments on this project would give a unique return - by way of solving many issues relating to the mystic curiosity of the human psyche.

The project attracted enormous publicity, almost completely dwarfing all the other important events that were taking place around the world at the time. It was difficult to find anybody who did not know about the moon signal. Even children in pre-schools were talking about and drawing pictures relating to the moon signal and the gossip around it. The entire population of the world was impatient to know more.

First Exploration ••• ••••

NASA scientists responded with speed, no delay whatsoever was allowable in design, planning, manufacture and follow up on all activities necessary to expedite the dispatch of the two satellites to take up moon orbit. After 13 months of hard work, NASA successfully launched the two satellites; one after the other within the time span of a day. Five days after the launch, NASA ground controllers maneuvered the satellites into the two Luna-stationery points as planned. The preparatory works on the 'messaging network' to transmit and receive the intermediate signals were also completed faultlessly.

However, all the hard work, enthusiasm and heightened expectations of the NASA and SETI Institute staff saw the same disappointment that was faced during the trails of the first exploration satellite. No signal. This time perhaps even more as the eighth day followed the seventh with 'no result'. Checking and re-checking of the coordinates of the previously established location, repeated testing of the instruments and computer programs, all proved fruitless. The Eighth day with 'no result' had set off a freeze within the NASA-SETI Institute group as well as the enthusiastic public. As the news was aired, most people in the world, especially the science community who anticipated new discoveries from this exploration were utterly disappointed. As had happened before, critics blamed various institutions for wasting money. Accusation that the entire project was a hoax was prevalent competing with a view that the aliens adopted radio silence to avoid detection. However NASA kept on without interruption to look for a signal. They were very hopeful of detecting it again as their first satellite launched a year ago, had positively established the existence of the signal. For SETI Institute staff who were well experienced in exercising patience, the "silence" of the past eight days was not a big issue. They still had not given up hope of picking up the signal again. On the 11th day their luck turned, they detected the signal. Hurray! A wild swing of emotions, - a swift change of mood, no more tiredness; alertness everywhere, many an eye filled with tears of joy. TV stations stopped all their regular broadcasts and flashed the news on the moon signal. People at offices stopped their work and logged onto the internet or tuned into their radios or rushed to the closest TV screen to know more about the exhilarating news.

The signal received was in a very steady stream and the receiver station on earth was able to record all the data coming directly from the moon source. Indication that coded information was embedded in the signal was quite strong. The media could not present much detail to the public other than stating that the satellite had detected an alien signal and it was ongoing. TV stations broadcast a few pictures of the moon taken by the satellite showing the area from which the signal emanated. For the people it was merely one more familiar picture of the moon's surface. The live TV broadcast continued in some channels with technical experts and non-experts commenting on the hypothetical possibilities related to the mystery. Unfortunately this exciting period did not last long. The signal lasted 1 hour and 12 minutes without break and ceased abruptly. Everybody wondered why, Nobody could come up with a reason. The signal did not appear thereafter. Attempts to re-establish contact with the signal were continued over a long time with no luck.

Having worked together for very many years, all the prominent scientists at the SETI Institute and NASA were by now, one big coherent family. They had been living and breathing these developments, successes and failures together. Though they did not have a definite explanation as to what had happened to the signal, many opinions were tabled for discussion and evaluation. One of the scientists was investigating if there were some sort of relationship amongst the dates on which the signal was detected. By developing and running a special computer program that he had developed to study this fact, it was discovered that the days on which the signal was detected in the past, fell into a mathematical linear series of fourteen. Based on this finding, he predicted that there was a great likelihood that the signal would reappear on the fourteenth day after the previous encounter. The tension was mounting at SETI-NASA center on the thirteenth day as they had not detected a signal up to then. All eyes, ears, hearts and the instruments were keenly focused from the very first second of the fourteenth day.

Bingo!

What great joy! The monitoring satellite received the signal a few hours after the dawn of the fourteenth day. It was the "Eureka!" moment. Everybody was thrilled. The scientist who made this exceptionally smart discovery was congratulated for his brilliant prediction. NASA was once again busy in getting on with their work. As noted in the first mission, the signal ceased abruptly after about an hour. Receipt of the signal became a common occurrence thereafter on every fourteenth day. Each time it only lasted around one hour to one and a half hours. The team presumed that the fourteen day signal cycle could be something to do with the twenty eight day cycle of the moon. But none of the team members were able to come up with a specific reason to explain this occurrence.

Now the main interest was to figure out who or what it was that was sending the signal and what information there was in the signal. The fourteen day signal cycle brought in more curiosity as it implied it was a planned signal rather than a randomly generated one. The scientists had come to believe that the signal had some form of coded information though they were unable to actually break the code.

The media had all manner of stories associated with the signal by this time. These stories originated both from the general public as well as world renowned intellectuals including space scientists. Programs and articles published through the mass media indicated that there could be highly intelligent people living in the moon's underground. One group of scientists stated that these signal waves could be a result of hither to unknown geological activity from within the moon. They connected their reasoning to the moon's rotation around the earth on a 28 day cycle. Some geologists even produced mathematical formulae to prove this hypothesis and published papers for consideration of the scientific community. Another explanation was that the radio waves could have been set off by creatures like electric eels living underground in the moon. There were also those who suggested that massive rivers and living colonies existed in the moon's underground. The organizations affiliated in supporting the concept of UFOs, opined that the signals were sent out by alien established radio stations and suggested the possibility of aliens living on the moon. This multitude of ideas established undeniably the abiding interest of the general public. Everybody who had been following this was quite unable to have peace of mind due to the mystic implications of the findings. This is how our mind works – we need to have answers to nagging mystic questions. The enormous urge many had was to know the reason for this fourteen day interruption of the signal and whether there was somebody behind its transmission.

NASA-SETI Institute was able to detect the signal on every 14th day without exception. Most times the signal lasted around one hour while on some days it lasted for up to one and a half hours. The shortest time was 23 minutes. The information coded in the signal had been similar all the time. The team was quite convinced that the codes were not randomly generated. In other words, it appeared that the signal was definitely from a stable source and the information was coded to denote something or had some specific purpose. Four months had now elapsed after the first detection of the fortnightly signal by the monitoring satellite. During these four months, recording of the signal and regular analysis of the data obtained was carried out continually. But to compound the mystery, there was no breakthrough in decoding of the data. The team of experts did not have any leading clues to proceed.

Future Exploration Missions Planning ••• ••••

The NASA-SETI Institute team was contemplating the steps that should be taken next. Considering the unexpected level of global support forthcoming, it was apparent that financing of another additional stage to "Know more about the moon signal - Project" would not be a problem. The task was to determine the "optimal" next step to implement. As many suggested, the best option would be sending of a manned probe. But it would be ten years down the line. An accelerated program of eight years was a possibility for a manned probe, but at an enormously increased cost. The other counter suggestion was to take up the whole issue for a comprehensive review in the first place. After detailed study, analysis and brain storming a broad proposal was brought up for discussion. This was a proposal structured with the idea of implementing the exploration mission in three phases.

Phase 1 planning, evolved to the use of two new satellites. One new satellite would be equipped with advanced instruments of receiving and transmitting capabilities and replace the existing satellite which was in L2 position in Luna-stationary orbit. The second new satellite would be placed in a low altitude orbit for reconnaissance purposes. The first satellite was to interact with the source and attempt to elicit a response to a radio signal beamed to it. If the signals detected earlier by earth were originated by intelligent beings, they might respond or react to the signals beamed by the satellite. The low orbital satellite was chiefly to be deployed to perform various reconnaissance tasks around the vicinity of the signal location. This satellite was to have capabilities of communicating with the first satellite when it was moving above the far side of the moon and of communicating with the satellite at L4 when it was moving above the near side of the moon.

The team thought that they could come up with some simple signal coding system, which could be transmitted to the moon source, to convey that another party was trying to communicate with it. In a nutshell, this was the principal idea, however it needed pooling of a wide range of expertise to formulate a workable plan covering all the different aspects that were necessary to be addressed. The time frame estimate for the phase 1 plan including the necessary satellite launch time was in the region of fourteen months.

Phase 2, involved sending a probe like the Mars Rover, that could scout around the area of the signal generation point and get a close up look at the signal transmitting area by employing several types of remote sensing devices. This probe was to have a high powered mast type drill capable of drilling down to a depth of 100 feet below the moon's surface while also being separately equipped with compact ultra-sonic instruments to study the sub-surface conditions on the moon. However, the specific research and investigating capabilities of the probe were to be reviewed (and expanded if necessary), close to the time of its component development and assembly, by the team of experts selected to work out the specifics. Most of the team members who were involved in the successful Mars Probes Projects (Spirit and Opportunity) were invited and readily agreed to head the team functions to take over the Phase 2 planning, design and implementation. NASA-SETI Institute officials expected that the outcome of Phase 1 of the project would provide the Phase 2 team with clues for reviewing, decision making and perfecting their objectives. The timeline for Phase 2 was set at twenty two months.

Phase 3, comprised landing a manned craft similar to Apollo 17 with a moon rover to drive around the signal area. Addition of a moon rover was an obvious choice though details were very sketchy at this stage. Phase 3 plans were confined to a very broad spectrum of ideas only. The team understood that this was at least ten years down the line. However, The NASA-SETI Institute team jointly decided that they should commence on all the preliminary planning and design tasks immediately. The NASA-SETI Institute team anticipated referring to the Phase 1 and Phase 2 findings at an appropriate juncture of the Phase 3 works to ensure refinement of the final form and scope of the project. Phase 1 and Phase 2 findings would dictate the changes to be made to the designs and operational segments of the Phase 3 tasks or might even lead to the complete abandoning of Phase 3 works, if the signal turned out to be nothing more than 'cosmic noise' or had no merit to make further endeavor worthwhile.

After the decision was made to proceed with the project it was inaugurated formally with very much emphasis placed on conforming to the planned target dates for each segment of activity.

Phase 1 project work was already underway in the designing of the two satellites; one with receiving and transmitting capability to 'communicate' with the moon signal source and the other low orbital one for reconnaissance tasks. As the L2 position that was vertically above the signal was to be occupied by this new satellite, the earlier monitoring satellite would be directed to fire its rockets to drift out of orbit and crash into a 'debris' spot on the near side of the moon. The 'crash' procedure was to be initiated twelve days ahead of the Phase 1 launch. The existing second satellite - the one with the line of sight from earth at the equilibrium position of L4 could however continue to function as the "Relay Unit". It had all the tracking hardware, jets to adjust its orientation etc. and the necessary transponders for communication with the Phase 1 satellite as well as the earth station. It had sufficient solar supplementation of battery power to work for over fifteen years. The team was more than confident that this arrangement would work without any technical glitches. Due to the re-usability of this satellite, the work involved reduced considerably and also helped to suppress additional expenditure. However, the replacement satellite at the far side at L2 would have to be larger, with additional propellant storage tanks and somewhat added features of a much larger Photo Voltaic array especially to supply the energy required to transmit highly penetrative and intense radio waves. While Phase 2 and Phase 3 project works were mostly restricted to the drawing boards, The Phase 1 part of the project was on the fast track and being carried through smoothly and without delay. A separate team was deployed to develop a language communications system to interact with the moon's signal source. Initially they suggested something similar to "Morse code" however, later, during brain storming sessions, it was realized that Morse code was too complicated for easy comprehension as it was associated with a particular (English) language. As such, a need was seen for the basis of signaling to be developed in a form independent of human language. The communications system had to have characteristics to teach the receiver that someone was trying to communicate with them. Also, it had to be simple to enable the receiver to understand the message quickly and transmit back its responses in an appropriate mode. If on basic interaction it was seen that there was a measure of even faltering understanding, the fundamental focus was to have adequate flexibility to develop a two way communication process that both parties could understand. The most important thing was to make it as simple as possible.

Public Response and Interesting Moon Facts ••• ••••

With time, peoples' enthusiasm blew the incident of the 'fortnightly signal' and the forthcoming exploration missions completely out of proportion. Enthusiastic groups including university students made documentary videos illustrating the possible eventualities that we could expect to encounter in the planned exploration. These documentaries contained all manner of imaginary and also mystic scenarios that people could think up. Some of these were very scientific and creative and even threw up ideas that were adopted into the Phase 2 and Phase 3 project thinking. As stated earlier, very many people strongly believed in the possibility of the existence of intelligent beings on the moon. Some people argued that they could be just like human beings. Others said such a possibility could never be and that they would be like the Martian figures that are shown on the cover pages of novels and characters in science fiction movies. The apparel market was flooded with items depicting diverse types of pictures in various colors, patterns and sizes. Especially the youth and children adored these garments. Online sales of the garments were booming. The internet was full of new web sites and blogs covering the subject of living beings on the moon.

Lunar geology became one of the prime subjects of study, attracting fresh attention of the scientific community. Many articles appeared in the media re-presenting and supplementing the details that were already known to man. To mention a few: The moon is as old as the earth; The lunar landscape is characterized by their ejecta, a few hills, and depressions filled by magma; Most areas are thought to have been formed by lava filled land with hills and valleys; Scientists have estimated that the Moon is twice as far away from the Earth now as it was 4 billion years ago; The moon's core is still molten; There are many craters; The deepest has been named after Isaac Newton and the depth from peak to floor of this crater is 29,000 feet. Though people knew more about the craters and other geological aspects of the moon's surface, knowledge of the substrate was extremely limited.

In 1962, scientist Dr. Gordon MacDonald stated, "If the astronomical data are analytically investigated, it is found that the data require the interior of the moon to be more like a hollow than a homogeneous sphere." And Nobel chemist Dr. Harold Urey suggested that there were many, large areas within the Moon that were simply "cavities." MIT's Dr.

Sean C. Solomon wrote, "the Lunar Orbiter experiments vastly improved our knowledge of the moon's gravitational field . . . indicating the frightening possibility that the moon might be hollow". When objects impact on it, the moon reverberates like a bell - supporting the contention of hollowness - though it may not actually be so. On March 7th, 1971, instruments placed on the lunar surface by the astronauts recorded a vapor cloud of water passing across the surface of the moon. This cloud movement lasted 14 hours and covered an area of about 100 square miles.

The Moon has a very weak magnetic field. This magnetic field is actually due to the moon rocks and is not related to the metallic core. Moon rocks are found to be magnetized and the exact reason for this has not been established. After hundreds of years of detailed observation and study, the Moon unfortunately continues to remain an enigma. Six moon landings and hundreds of experiments resulted in raising more questions than answers. Some of the moon's craters originated internally, yet there is no indication that the moon was ever hot enough to produce volcanic eruptions for these craters to arise.

The following documented facts about the Moon are presented to broaden understanding of it.

- The Moon has a diameter of 2,160 miles and orbits the Earth at a mean distance of 238,857 miles. It orbits the Earth in 27.322 days, and always keeps the same side facing the Earth.

- Because of the lack of an atmosphere, the temperature of the Moon's surface varies between -180°C and +110°C.

- The moon's centre of mass is about 6000 feet closer to the Earth than its geometric centre (which should cause wobbling during rotation), but actually the moon's bulge based on shape is on the far side of the moon, away from the Earth.

- Hundreds of "moonquakes" are recorded each year that cannot be attributed to meteor impacts. In November, 1958, Soviet astronomer Nikolay A. Kozyrev of the Crimean Astrophysical Observatory photographed a gaseous eruption on the moon near the crater Alphonsus. He also detected a reddish glow that lasted about an hour. In 1963, astronomers at the Lowell Observatory also saw reddish glows on the crests of ridges in the Aristarchus region. These observations have proved to be precisely identical and periodical, in repeating sequence as the moon moves cyclically slightly closer and farther away from the Earth. These do not seem to be natural phenomena.

- Mascons are large, dense, circular masses, lying twenty to forty miles beneath the centers of each of the moon's large maria (dried crater-like ocean beds). Some scientists suggest that these are broad, disk-shaped objects that could even be some kind of artificial construction. It is claimed that large circular disks would not appear perfectly centered beneath each huge mare by coincidence or accident.

- On November 20th, 1969, the Apollo 12 crew jettisoned the lunar module ascent stage causing it to crash onto the moon. The Lunar Module's impact (about 40 miles from the Apollo 12 landing site) set off an artificial moonquake of startling characteristics - the moon reverberated like a bell for more than an hour. This phenomenon was repeated with Apollo 13 (intentionally commanding the third stage to impact on to the moon), with even more startling results. Seismic instruments recorded that the reverberations lasted for three hours and twenty minutes and traveled downward to a depth of twenty-five miles, leading to the conclusion that the moon has an unusually light core or even no-core at all.

- The moon's crust is much harder than presumed. Remember the extreme difficulty the astronauts encountered when they tried to drill into the maria? Surprised! The maria is composed primarily of ilmenite, a mineral which contains a large amount of titanium, the same metal used to fabricate the hulls of deep-diving submarines and the skin of the SR-71 "Blackbird". Uranium 236 and neptunium 237 (elements not found in nature on Earth) were discovered in lunar rocks, as were rustproof iron particles. While some argue that these are the result of volcanic activity, 'hollow-mooners' say that this is proof that the interior of the moon was hollowed out by artificial means.

- The moon's mean density is 3.34 gm/cm3 whereas the Earth's mean density is 5.5 gm/cm3. What does this mean? Nobel chemist Dr. Harold Urey suggested that the moon's reduced density could arise from large cavities inside the moon.

- MIT's Dr. Sean C. Solomon wrote, "the Lunar Orbiter experiments vastly improved our knowledge of the moon's gravitational field... indicating the frightening possibility that the moon might be hollow."

- Ours is the only moon in the solar system with a near-perfect circular orbit of equal orbital and spin speeds. "Something" put the moon in orbit with its precise altitude, course, and speed.

- As outrageous as the Moon-Is-a-Spaceship theory is, all of the above facts attain perfect harmony if one assumes that the moon is a gigantic extraterrestrial craft, brought here eons ago by intelligent beings. This is the only theory that is supported by all of the data, and there are no data that contradict this theory.

- NASA, one year before the first lunar landing, reported 570+ lights and flashes on the moon from 1940 to 1967. Operation Moon Blink: NASA's Operation Moon Blink detected 28 lunar events in a relatively short period of time.

- Lunar Bridge: On July 29, 1953, John J. O'Neill observed a 12-mile-long bridge straddling the crater Mare Crisium. Later in August, British astronomer Dr. H.P. Wilkens verified its presence, "It looks artificial. It's almost incredible that such a thing could have been formed in the first instance, or if it was formed, could have lasted during the ages in which the moon has been in existence

- The Shard: The Shard, an obelisk-shaped object that towers 1½ miles from the Ukert area of the moon's surface, was discovered by Orbiter 3 in 1968. Dr. Bruce Cornet, who studied the amazing photographs, stated, "No known natural process can explain such a structure."

- The Obelisks: Lunar Orbiter II took several photographs in November 1966 that showed several obelisks, one of which was more than 150 feet tall. "The spires were arranged in precisely the same way as the apices of the three great pyramids."

- The Tower: One of the most curious features ever photographed on the Lunar surface is an amazing spire that rises more than 5 miles from the Sinus Medii region of the lunar surface.

- On Earth and in the composition of other planets, the heavier elements are normally found in the core while the lighter materials are concentrated at the surface. But not so with the Moon. The abundance of refractory elements like titanium in the surface areas is so pronounced, that several geologists proposed that the refractory compounds must have been brought to the moon's surface in great quantity in some unknown way. They are adamant. They don't know how, but there is no other way for this to have happened!

- In 2009 NASA confirmed abundance of water deposits on the moon

Back to the Moon Project ••• ••••

As time passed, the Phase 1 satellite program was seen to be making smooth, steady and rapid progress. The replacement satellite was given the name "Hi!" as its purpose was to say "Hi" to the moon signal source with the hope of a positive response. The reconnaissance satellite was named "Buddy" and the "Relay" or "Go-Between-Unit" at L4 was named "GBU".

Though a range of possible alternatives was rigorously evaluated, the experts were unable to come up with an easy to implement "Language" or system to communicate with the signal source. However, as a basic first step, capabilities were incorporated into the satellites to produce basic "dot" and "dash" signals. The team's intention was to start with a simple system using these signals and to scale it up to an advanced mode depending on the actual needs that might arise. The computer in the satellite had built-in capability to cater to such needs. The necessary upgrading programs were to be uploaded from NASA control center as and when required. Many advanced technologies that NASA acquired from the Mars programs were used extensively. The team decided to restrict their initial signal bursts to "dot", "dot", "dot" and "dot", "dot", "dot", "dot" patterns (••• ••••) as they thought these two sequences would be sufficient to attract attention if there were any intelligent beings to interpret them. These were akin to someone knocking at the door. If one were paying attention, it would be very simple to understand that it was a deliberate call. In Morse code, the "dot", "dot", "dot" sequence is "S" and "dot", "dot", "dot", "dot" is "H", but these were not relevant considerations at all as the basic idea was different in this case. In fact the team thought this would be the simplest form in which intelligent beings could respond to indicate that they had 'heard' the signal. The frequency and bandwidth of the radio signal to be transmitted was chosen to have the same value as the frequency of the moon signal. The satellite also carried a LASER beam generator which could create and transmit the same "dot" and "dash" message bursts to the moon's signal source. This was suggested at a later stage for incorporation into the designs as an alternative method of communicating with the signal source. The team believed that this could come in handy as absolutely nothing was known about the Moon's signal source. Some team members opined that if the moon signal was produced by living beings, then the LASER signal would have a greater chance of drawing their attention than a radio signal, due to its visibility. The LASER beam was designed to have a diameter around 0.3 inches.

All these preparatory tasks and many other details of this mission were not at all unknown to the public due to the wide and persistent media coverage. Details were disseminated especially through the internet and televised documentary programs. The SETI-NASA joint website updated their information daily, indicating the latest status of the special events and other interesting things that were happening around the project. Meanwhile there was no disruption in receipt of the regular moon signal. Like the rising of the sun every morning, without default, the signal was received on every fourteenth day. The data that reached the earth through the existing two satellites had the same unvarying radio characteristics. In spite of long expert hours spent, the intelligence encoded in the signal was still a mystery and resisted all attempts at decoding. As time passed, to everybody's disappointment, almost all the scientists working on the signal were inclined to conclude reluctantly that there was nothing more they could do. However, they still held on to the belief that the coding pattern in the signal was not randomly generated, but had a specific purpose.

The final week for the Phase 1 satellite's launch arrived almost unnoticed by all but the few engaged in de-activating and jettisoning the first monitoring satellite at L2. As explained earlier this had to be done eight to twelve days ahead to make way for the larger and smarter replacement satellite "cousin Hi". Time had indeed passed very, very quickly. The rocket carrying the satellites "Hi" and "Buddy" lifted off from the Kennedy space center without a glitch. Both satellites were ensconced in the same rocket and would be launched into their individual trajectories later on. As expected, full TV coverage and publicity was a feature of this event. Public interest was enormous and insatiable. It would take another four to five days to position "Hi" at the correct moon orbit and at the exact pre-defined spot occupied by its predecessor. The team in charge of Buddy waited for day 3 to separate "Buddy" from "Hi" and locate Buddy in its own independent trajectory.

Satellites are most easily put into the moon's orbit by using the gravitational pull of the moon. When this is done, the satellite goes into an elliptical orbit first. To change the elliptical orbit to a circular orbit many small and gradual adjustments are required. The NASA ground control station commands small onboard rockets on the satellite to fire and adjust the orbital path. These rockets are fired when the satellite is at apogee or the pointed part of the ellipse which is its most distant point from the moon. Applying rocket thrust thus in the direction of the flight path makes the perigee or flattish part of the ellipse which is its nearest point to the moon, to move further out and makes the ellipse shaped orbit get more rounded. By repeating this procedure a few times, NASA was able to gradually nudge the new satellites into circular orbits and then position them at the exact Luna-Synchronous point for "Hi" and at the chosen precise orbit that "Buddy" was to occupy. However, there were two more days for the scheduled 14th day moon signal. During this waiting period SETI-NASA linked the new satellite with the other Luna-stationary satellite "GBU" that had line of sight with earth. This was already in place from the earlier mission. The course adjustments required were a bare minimum to interlink the communication systems together. The team in charge of "Buddy" handled their task of maintaining it in its orbit flawlessly and ensured that it stayed linked to both "Hi" and "GBU". "Buddy" commenced its tasks as soon as it was settled in, in its 'patrolling' orbit. Already, the SETI-NASA team was looking at some high definition pictures "Buddy" had relayed back to earth. Meanwhile, the team in charge of "Hi" was busy testing all the vital instruments to ensure that they were all in optimal working condition. Several test signal busts were fired at the

Moon's signal area, back and forth from earth to the satellites to verify that all systems were fully functional.

Using prior records, SETI-NASA predicted the time that the moon signal could be expected. The countdown started. The moment arrived to receive the signal. As predicted and now expected, the signal was received within a time deviation of less than 5 minutes. "Hi" was now picking up the signal and the staff at SETI-NASA center exploded with cheers, smiles and high fives. SETI-NASA spent the next fifteen minutes in tweaking the instruments to achieve the highest possible level of refinement and clarity of communication.

This time, a lot was expected from the mission!

The Moon ••• ••••

Here is some news that will take you very, very much by surprise.

It would not be proper to keep you guessing any further. Here it is!

"The moon is another world inhabited with humans".

Can you believe it? Yes, this is the truth!

In the moon, the "people" do not live above or on the ground as we do on earth but down below under the surface. They live in an enormous inner space naturally formed as a labyrinth of gigantic caves below the surface crust. The surface crust forms the roof of the caves and varies in thickness from a lower limit around three feet up to a maximum reaching a hundred feet. In spite of the many manned missions to the moon, nobody was able to discover the fact that the moon was the closest world to earth with a wide variety of life forms, including people in very many ways similar to us. These people have been living sub-terra or underground in the moon for millions of years. They also arrived at their present form after going through an evolutionary process similar to what took place on earth. They encountered as well, causes to form 'disproportionate' sized brains like us with resulting ability to develop tools and establish skills in scientific inquiry, discovery and formulation of the laws of nature. Marconi's investigations resulted in the discovery and use of radio waves on earth in 1895. The people in the moon have only just begun to experiment with and arrived at the first stage of creating and transmitting radio waves of a significant intensity. The situation of moon scientists in the context of discovering radio waves, right at present, is very similar to the situation that the scientists on earth were in when they discovered radio waves. They did not know what it was or have any idea of what to do with it. According to historical records there have been many interesting incidents associated with new discoveries on the earth. In most cases the people who made such discoveries were overwhelmed and confused by their findings. The moon scientists might have been in similar situations, as many times. As a comparison of the technical capabilities of the moon people with ours, it would not be wrong to say that they are only about a few hundred years behind us. This comparison is valid only in the area of knowledge of science and not in other areas such as their traits etc. Their social structure and behavioral traits are unimaginably different from those of the people on earth.

The news of people living in the moon will cause a barrage of questions to arise in everyone's mind. The following segments of this narration are an attempt to answer some of the common questions readers would have.

The moon's internal geological structure is very strange and unique. It has vast areas of hollow underground caves. This is because the moon passed through boiling and molten states before it cooled down to its stable present day temperature. Some caves are miles and miles in length and breath. The heights from floor to roof inside these caves range from several feet to hundreds of feet. These caves exist at varying depths below the moon's surface. However, variations in thickness of the top roof cover of the caves are very large from cave to cave in a somewhat random fashion. Some caves are only a few feet below the moon's surface and some are a few hundreds of feet below. Almost all the caves are internally connected to each other and it is possible to trace many paths through interconnected caves to fully 'circumnavigate' the moon without ever stepping out on to its outer surface. The tops of the caves that form the crust of the moon's surface are supported on massive vertical rock pillars that rise out of the bottom surface or base of the caves. These vertical support structures are very hard and rocklike and naturally contoured in shell like formations endowing them with heavy load bearing capabilities. The cave system is integrally connected all along the moon's subsurface thus providing ample stability, strength and structural integrity, to sustain surface impacts resulting from falling meteorites or similar space objects. To visualize the interior of these caves a comparable earth structure would be the NFL football domes. They would compare in size with some of the smaller caves but none of the caves in the moon are formed in a particular shape, pattern, length, breadth or height, and are quite irregular in shape. Surface terrain is also to a large extent irregular and .variable, however vast flat areas are also found at many locations.

To review some of the facts given earlier about the moon, there are many references to the hollowness of the moon. As an example, re-read the following; "On November 20, 1969, the Apollo 12 crew jettisoned the lunar module ascent stage causing it to crash onto the moon. The Lunar Module's impact (about 40 miles from the Apollo 12 landing site) created an artificial moonquake with startling characteristics - the moon reverberated like a bell for more than an hour. This phenomenon was repeated with Apollo 13 (by intentionally commanding the third stage to impact on to the moon), with even more startling results. Seismic instruments recorded that the reverberations lasted for three hours and twenty minutes and traveled down to a depth of twenty-five miles, thus leading to the conclusion that the moon has an unusually light core or even none at all". This is concrete proof of the real status of the moon's internal structure, though scientists on earth could not realize this fact even after landing twelve people on the moon since 1969.

Here's more!

Many surface crusts are made of a material known as lunar regolith. Lunar regolith transforms into translucent forms through a process called agglutination when the regolith is subjected to high heat. In many places, parts of the moon's surface consist of translucent material embedded in the moon's outer crust. These surfaces allow a substantial degree of sunlight to penetrate into the caves. Most of this glass like surface material has been naturally formed, millions of years ago. Amongst the translucent surface areas, there are also many areas of near clear-glass transparency. Some of these areas are vast to the extent of spreading over several square miles. Though these large transparent areas are very limited compared to the total surface area of the moon, moon astronomers of the caliber of Galileo Galilei, have been using these windows as gateways to observe objects in outer space. Nevertheless, their knowledge of the planetary system and universe is very limited and cannot be compared to the discoveries made by Galileo. These moon astronomers can probably be compared to people on earth around 600 to 1000 years ago, who were interested in the heavenly bodies.

Due to refraction of the sunlight that penetrates into the caves, massive rainbow like color beams frequently appear in very many places inside the caves. Due to the vastness and the complexity of the spectrum of rainbow colors intermingling with each other, there is a stunningly beautiful visual effect inside the caves. The glow from the moon's outer surface when seen from inside the caves, gives a further dimension of beauty for the visual enjoyment of the people of the moon. However, where there are no transparent cave roof surfaces, the caves are gloomy and would be pitch dark if not for a small amount of light reaching them from adjacent caves.

Just as happens on the earth, the sunlight that penetrates through the transparent crust helps the growth of vegetation in the caves to a substantial extent. However sunlight is not the main light source in the caves. These sources are described later. The types of vegetation found in the moon are markedly different from the ones on earth. The plants commonly seen in the caves are quite short and look very much like the miniature trees, bushes and shrubs grown using Japanese "Bonsai" techniques. The total range of plant varieties does not exceed 5000 different types.

Though the moon has no atmosphere on the outside, the caves are filled with 'air' well suited to supporting the respiratory needs of life forms. Surprisingly, 90% percent of the moon's internal atmosphere comprises oxygen which exceeds the corresponding oxygen proportion in the earth's atmosphere. The moon's internal atmosphere also contains significant quantities of carbon dioxide, nitrogen, sulfur dioxide, methane and a very small quantity of other gases. The eco-system sustaining life is different to that on earth. The moon's cave system is not fully hermetically sealed as there are openings from the caves leading to the moon's outer surface. But these openings are few in number. The people of the Moon are well aware of the barren, austere conditions and the life threatening dangers on the moon's surface. As very orderly and self-disciplined citizens or as their brains have been programmed to do so, the people of the moon always keep away from those egresses and never attempt to go out to explore the outer surface.

Similar to the great lakes in North America, there are massive lakes in the hollow underground cave system. However unlike the great lakes, the caves roofs over the lakes of the moon are supported by the natural array of vertical pillars protruding through the waters like a massive cluster of Mangrove roots. The underside of the roof above the lakes and also the vertical pillars protruding through the waters are 'coated' by a gel like material. This gel shows many of the signs of being a living substance. It also emits light and carries out the function of 'cleaning' the moon's atmosphere by absorbing impurities which it assimilates as a nutrient. It rejects some part of the absorbed impurities as balls of waste exited into the lakes. The waste in turn is eaten by the fish or absorbed by plants in the lakes. The reflection of the softly glowing gel on the water enhances the lighting in the area of the lakes. At all places in the moon, the water in the lakes is clean, not salty and is suited for use directly for drinking. The waters of these lakes are however subject to massive tidal effects. These are due to the fluctuation of the resultant of the gravitational tugs of the earth and the sun as the earth spinning on its own axis and carrying the moon in orbit in turn orbits the sun. Because of the low moon gravity, the tidal effects are checked weakly and the water levels rise and fall by hundreds of feet. The tides force the water to spread hundreds of miles along the vast underground areas thus wetting the dry areas of the caves in a cyclic pattern. Because of these vast latitudinal and longitudinal fluctuations of water spread, there are artificial water stream formations all over the geological-structure of the moon. The streams of water flow over the cave surfaces and create huge waterfalls at some places. These waterfalls last for many days and appear and disappear in a cyclic pattern, following the tides. Rounded boulders can be seen all over the streams, indicating that they have been subjected to heavy erosion over millions of years. The water streams formed below the sub grade of the caves cause the formation of complex hydro geological patterns. Depending on the moon's geological conditions at each specific spot, the complexity of the hydrogeology varies from location to location.

The age and composition of the lunar geology is somewhat similar to that of the earth. But unlike the earth's crust, the moon's crust is stable and does not rest on a moving set of Tectonic plates. No active volcanoes are found on the moon; but there are many hot spots located throughout the bottom surfaces of the caves, indicating the closeness of those spots to the molten inner core of the moon. Due to the fully enclosed nature of the cave system, the cave interior always features high humidity.

The temperatures around the equatorial and mid latitude surface at daytime and in the night are around 225°F and minus 298°F respectively. This is a very wide temperature range. The temperatures at the bottom of the craters and the areas of the craters in shadow are extremely low. In fact there are hyper-cool areas featuring Arctic conditions. As the moon day is approximately 28 earth days, heating and cooling of the moon's surfaces affects the inside cave temperature significantly. For example, when one side of the moon's surface receives direct sun light for 14 earth days (say the east side), the opposite side (i.e. the west side) reaches a minimum temperature of minus 298 degrees Fahrenheit. As a result of having these huge temperature differences for very long periods of time, the interior of the caves get either cooled or heated correspondingly. The lakes in some of these areas are permanently frozen. The temperature difference in the opposite side of the moon makes the air in the cave move from one area (east side) to the other (west side) creating complex wind movements. When high speed wind flows across the vertical rock structures, it makes gurgling sounds in the caves, resulting in eerie or weird echo effects. The blowing wind helps to mitigate the high humidity conditions in the caves to some extent. It is known that the tops of a few craters situated at the lunar South Pole receive sunlight almost totally uninterruptedly. Due to this fact, people on earth have identified these as the ideal areas in which to establish bases on the moon, if they would ever be able to do so.

Many gigantic meteorite impacts on the moon have created massive craters that can be seen from the earth. Most of the major impacts have taken place millions of years ago. Some of these impacts have left devastating effects on the cave system. When such impacts created deep craters, sometimes the depths of these crates reached even below the water levels of the lakes in the sub-surface of the moon. When this happened, the water from the lakes gushed into the low level areas to fill them up instantaneously. However, when this water got exposed to very low temperatures the water transformed into solid ice. Once the ice formed, it remained as ice permanently. The surfaces of some craters never get sunlight as they are permanently shielded by the shadows of the mountains around them. These craters sustain hyper cool temperatures. On the other hand, even if the sunlight falls onto the bottoms of the craters, the heat delivered by the sun is not sufficient to melt the ice. Many deep places in the moon's craters have permanent layers of ice. The self-sealing effect of caves by the water as explained above helps to maintain the integrity of the cave system, preventing large quantities of air escaping to the surface. Millions of years ago, there may have been occurrences of large quantities of air escaping from the caves due to meteorite damage. However the present cave structure has retained the cave atmosphere intact for thousands of years without any major leakage. The quantum of oxygen generated by the plants might probably be sufficient to make up for the proportion leaking out to the exterior.

As is the case on the earth, the moon is also a habitat for mammals, birds, fish, reptiles, amphibians, insects and other life forms. As direct sunlight does not fall into the caves in significant quantities, the eyes of all creatures including those of the humans are naturally evolved to possess the common attributes of nocturnal animals. Similar to the situation on the earth, the animals in tropical areas and in very cold areas of the moon have their own evolutionary traits adapted to the specific environment. The grazing mammal species are limited as grassy lands are not abundant. There are very many species of bats. Some are very much like the leaf-nosed bats and funnel-eared bats on earth. The bird population is abundant and diverse and is spread over more than 300 species. Most of these species are however very different from those found on the earth and are territorial. Many birds of species that can be taught to talk are kept as pets by the moon people.

This description has been restricted to a very brief outline as it would run into thousands of pages if all details of the moon animals were to be expressed here. However the following exceptional fact about a particular animal is worth stating. Just as on earth, there are a few varieties of primates that live in the caves. As with the moon people, the principal source of diet of these primates is the vegetation found in the lakes - as the leaves of shrubs and grasses in the savanna in the moon do not replenish rapidly unlike on the earth. Among the few species of primates on the moon, a very unusual species is the great ape as it uses a word based language to communicate. Though the anatomical structure of the larynges of the apes does not enable them to make the extensive range of sounds typical to the humans, this specific variety of ape is unique. They have over 70 words for vocalization and use them to communicate with each other. When they talk, the vocalized words are generally followed with supporting body gestures and hand movements to support the communication. Many of these words feature in their communications when they socialize or show affection and also are used to warn other members of the group of the approach of predators. When moon people use the apes' words to attempt to talk to the apes, the apes completely ignore the people and show no response whatever. It appears, this "pay no attention act" is a deliberate one as their body language and behavior indicate very clearly the message "we respect you; please mind your business; leave us alone". The moon people including the children understand this message very well and hence do not bully them. Contrasting with the tendency to ignore the moon people, if any food is offered by the moon people it is readily accepted as is typical of ape behavior. The clear difference between these apes and the apes on earth is that, as soon as they receive the food they gather into a group and share all the food amongst themselves, evidencing an extraordinary social trait not found in other animals. This might be a trait that these apes have inherited for their survival in the evolutionary process.

By nature, moon people are extremely kind and sensitive. They love and look after the animals. As on earth, the felines and other carnivorous animals kill and feed on other animals for their survival and without such a mode of interactive controls it might have been difficult to maintain balance in the moon's eco system.

The evolutionary process has produced many light producing creatures in the caves. These creatures are commonly found on lakes, on land and in the mountainous areas of the caves. Bioluminescent organisms in the moon are not at all similar to those on earth. They are much more efficient light producers. People living in the moon have found ways to promote the growth of bioluminescent organisms on a mass scale. Though not very significant in terms of contribution, these organisms are part of the light sources. People in the moon had also developed devices to divert the sunlight from the bright areas to many dark regions by ingenious light reflection methods. The scientists in the moon have made much progress in the field of photo-luminescent or glow in the dark material. Photo-luminescent products are very widely used for many purposes. Though their knowledge base is still not advanced to understand the atomic or molecular structures to analyze material in depth, the moon people have made significant advancements in materials' science by trial and error experimentation using naturally occurring substances as additives and pigments.

On a very much higher scale than all these light resources, the primary lighting source in the moon is a glowing, light emanating material that is unique to the moon. This material is quite unknown to the people on earth. It occurs as huge crystals called "Babaloniums". This material is not a science fiction precious material like the one that was seen in the movie "Avatar". This is a real natural substance and is found in many places in the moon. The moon people have been aware of the existence of this material for thousands of years. Other than the sunlight coming through the translucent moon surfaces, Babaloniums is the other major light producer in the caves specially to provide light during the night time of the moon which lasts 14 (earth) days. The moon people harvest the Babaloniums whenever they come across them. As these have been collected from wherever they were found, by their ancestors over thousands of years, new ones are usually only discovered by accident. The few discovered in the recent past were found near the narrow alley ways leading from the caves to the outside of the moon's surface. The enormous risks involved in venturing into these alleys, are a naturally discouraging factor in looking for new Babaloniums. Babaloniums usually occur in chunks ranging in weight from as little as 5 to as much as 100 pound crystals. The moon people have strategically positioned these glowing crystals to illuminate their cities and other public places. There is a unique way of activating the Babaloniums to produce light, as virgin Babaloniums material found in the ground does not glow at all. The process involves having direct sun light fall onto these crystals for a period of 2 to 3 days without interruption. At some point of the two to three day interval, the crystals get self-triggered and start to glow. At first the glow is quite faint, but the brightness keeps on increasing gradually on its own. Once the triggering has taken place, sunlight is no longer required. Within a few hours the crystals reach their maximum brightness which is very intense and penetrative. Once this stage is reached, the glowing becomes permanent and unvarying and seems to assume the status of an eternal light source. As such most of the Babaloniums providing light at present have been those collected over the past thousands of years. When moon people find non-glowing Babaloniums, the process of triggering them is within access without much difficulty; the secret of triggering has been passed on from generation to generation. However the moon people have not found any method of suspending or stopping the glow, other than by using an external barrier or covering to control the brightness. Babaloniums do not produce heat or any other form of energy - only light. There are naturally triggered Babaloniums crystals in many mountainous parts within the caves. Some of these locations are impossible to access, and hence one might wonder how these were triggered. Probably these areas would have somehow been exposed to sunlight thousands of years ago. These glowing bodies on the tops of distant cave mountains produce panoramic sceneries, emulating lighthouses and LASER shows on earth. The light that the Babaloniums emit varies from crystal to crystal but is mostly of pale blue or purple color. Though this material is very hard like diamond, if a big crystal is broken into small pieces, the glowing effect diminishes immediately. The moon people are aware of this. The reason for the glow in these amazing crystals may be linked to some form of high molecular weight radioactive material, but this is a mere assumption. The real reason is not known. People on earth would love to have the Babaloniums as it will make a true revolution in the lighting industry, as light no longer radiates from a filament or any other external energy source, but from the material itself. Just like sunlight, the lights produced by the Babaloniums assist the growth of vegetation in the habitat; especially the water plants that grow in the lakes.

The moon people have been using fire for thousands of years for cooking and lighting. Man-made lamps and torches are used for illuminating the dwellings and public areas as an additional light source. However, the total light produced by all the light sources mentioned above is nowhere close to the luminosity of the dimmest evening on earth. Probably the best light condition in the caves may be equated to the hazy light at late sunset during winter time. But living beings in the cave system including the people are so used to the low light conditions it is not an issue or a barrier to their daily activities.

The lakes are the main supporting source sustaining life in the moon. The lakes support an array of living organisms including fish of various varieties and some small sized aquatic mammals also, like on the earth. Only a limited range of water plants grow in the lakes and these are all found in all the lakes in the moon. The most abundant water plant variety resembles seaweeds, but is very much thicker and stronger than the earth's variety. These water plants which grow very rapidly and proliferate in vast quantities are the primary source of food and nutrient for the moon people.

Nitrogen rich minerals which are an essential component of nutrition of all moon organisms and also help in growth of the plants are recycled in the lakes by the cyclic tidal action that occurs. The moon people, process the water plants manually to make their food, various types of fabrics, building materials, fuel, construction materials etc. Trial and error procedures and intelligent projections over thousands of years have resulted in the development of techniques for utilization of these materials for a wide range of uses. The transport machinery such as boats, barges, carts etc., which are of simple basic shape and function are made of various categories of compounded raw materials developed from the water plants.

A type of Algae very similar to the blue green alga grows in abundance in the lakes. Strangely, the principal mechanism of the growth of the moon's algae is not photosynthesis, but the aquatic organisms living in the lakes. The alga communities grow in massive colonies which have the ability to enclose small aquatic organisms and absorb all the nutrients from the live microbial they prey on. This is comparable very closely with the processes adopted by carnivorous plants found on the earth. Because the alga cells have a special attribute of a very high ratio of surface-area-to-volume, they can absorb nutrients very quickly. Over the past thousands of years, moon people have developed techniques to extract oil from the algae. This oil serves a wide range of purposes depending on how it is processed and is used to make medicines, food, fuel for illumination and many other purposes as well.

Moon people have ingrained traits whereby they deeply care for the environment that they live in. They make a very thorough investigation of effects on the environment before embarking on any activity and they would never exploit the resources around them in a way that would disturb the ecosystem. Due to the very nature of their approach, the waste that they generate is a minimum and does not introduce any toxicity at all to the environment. Only a few different types of metals are known to the moon people. Metals are not extensively developed or widely used, unlike on earth.

The social behavior of moon people ••• ••••

The social structure of moon people is very vastly different to that of the people on the earth. The entire populations of moon people can be pictured as groups of hermits living in secluded massive enclosed habitats. They are extremely friendly to each other and socially predisposed to live a form of community life. Though different personalities exist, conflicts are extremely rare. They always have non-confrontational solutions to situations where seemingly opposing requirements arise and naturally respond to each other in such a manner as to leave no room for conflict. They are very united and work in harmony with each other as is seen on earth among the bees in a beehive. They care for each other and are fundamentally oriented only towards "purposes of the moment" and do not have long term plans. They share all possessions that they have with others as everybody owns everything and nobody owns anything. They seem like fun loving serious people. Moon people do not seem to possess anything other than a few personal effects.

Dating back to ancient days, they have a calendar, a written language and their own type of art and music. All aspects of the lives of moon people are governed by commonsense rules made known to them by the elders. These rules have been taught to them verbally for generations and are typically introduced during their childhood. Most governing principles have been in place for centuries without appreciable change. These guidelines have worked very well and are secular in nature and are not written down in any document as such. Forms of written books on various subjects exist at the academic facilities, but there are no books on rules for people to follow or for reference. The standard norms that all people ought to obey are well understood by all the moon people including the children. It seems as if they have been brain washed with all these ideas and behavioral patterns from their birth.

The children are nurtured in community based centers. The children from the level of infants are raised in these institutional centers. These are the day care centers, preschools, primary, secondary, high schools, colleges and research institutions in the moon; all in one single locality. Children at these centers treat all adults with utmost respect regarding them as mentors and as no different from their parents.

A more or less common sense approach is followed by the moon people in their day to day affairs. This helps to keep the harmony and close bonding of the community that they treasure very much. They always act on the principle of carrying out "What needs to be done?" at a particular moment and engage themselves promptly on such tasks rather than wait for someone to give directions. In instances, where guidance is necessary, it is the elders who provide it. Notwithstanding very minor personality differences amongst the elders, their basic or fundamental ideas are nearly identical. Conflicts never arise amongst the elders who are well recognized community leaders living like ordinary people, among the population. The leaders respect each other's seniority on the basis of their age or their knowledge on a particular subject. This is the principle they adopt whenever they encounter issues to determine who should take the key leadership decisions. In each city, there is a common place for the leaders to gather at when major issues come up for review.

The behavior of moon people if observed from outside, might appear to imitate the interaction of a number of pre-programmed robots working in harmony. There has never been any clash or differences amongst the moon people. Words such as fight and war do not exist in their vocabulary. Their lack of diversity is symbolized by the fact that they have only one style of clothing. Their dress is of very simple style covering the full body including the head, with face kept open. These clothes closely resemble the ceremonial Jedi robes seen in the Star Wars movies. Men, women and all children wear the same type of clothing. The color is desert sand brown. The fabrics for clothing are made of none other than the fiber extracted from the water plants that grow profusely in the lakes. The physical structures of men and women, very much resemble that of the people on earth. The entire population talks the same language. Men and women do not have hair on the head from birth. But the men have beards, but no mustaches. They are very fair in complexion, so much so, that most blood vessels can be seen through their skin. They walk in a swinging style, resembling chimpanzees walking upright. The women and men are treated equally though men have a slight edge over the women in leadership roles. Girls rarely seek to pursue higher studies or research assignments.

The entire cave dwelling system is made up of a very large number of cities. Distinct areas are demarcated for various community functions, community operations and dwellings within the cities. Neither money nor other form of currency is used among the moon people. There is no need to use money due to the way the community is structured to operate. Neither food nor other commonly used or consumable items belong to anyone specifically but to all the people, as was also set out in the well-known speech by the Native American or Red Indian Chief "Seattle" of America.

Food supplies come directly from various water plants that grow in the lakes in abundance. The moon people consume a mix of raw food as well as cooked food. The flowers, seeds, leaves, stems and the bulbs of the water plants are their staple diet. These foods contain all the proteins and other necessary ingredients necessary for healthy living. The water plants are processed in many ways to make a great variety of delicious cuisine. The moon people cultivate limited varieties of subsidiary food crops in the fields. They domesticate a cattle-like animal to obtain its milk. Ritualistically, when moon people drink milk, they practice a custom of kneeling down and chanting certain words and phrases. This ritual has the purpose of thanking the animal for providing the milk as well as to say sorry to the calves for taking part of their share of milk. The moon people are not meat eaters and are vegetarians. As such, they do not raise animals for meat. The specific reason why they do not eat meat is not known. However, taking life from any living creature is absolutely unthinkable for them. The children are taught to treat the animal that provided milk to them as of equal status as their own mothers who provided breast milk to them when they were babies.

Though a moon day is equivalent to 28 earth days, surprisingly, the biological day cycle of the moon people is 24 earth hours. This shows that their biological clock or the day cycle has nothing to do with the sun rise and sun set in the moon. Perhaps the 24 hour period of time is a unique biological 'interval of renewal' that nature has given to all human species. Usually moon people sleep about eight hours a day at "any time of convenience" and remain active during most of the remaining hours. The "time of convenience" varies for each individual. As a result of not having a particular day or night time, there are always people awake and active all of the time. Therefore, all community based activities take place all the time and continuously without stoppage. There are no holiday systems practiced in the moon. Every day is a working day and every hour is an active hour. Every hour is also a sleeping hour to whoever desires to consider it that way.

Births and deaths are considered natural events in life and hence emotional situations at the levels experienced on the earth are unknown in the moon. Burial of bodies takes place a few hours after death. The persons, who happen to be the companions of the dead person at the time of death, get the assistance of others in the vicinity to wrap the dead body in fabric as in mummified bodies and prepare for its burial in an assigned area. Sometimes, the graves are hand dug if the soil is sandy and burial takes place without any elaborate ceremonies. There are no eulogies. The moon people believe that all persons are equal and hence have no notion of high or low status in this regard, other than for the special respect that they have for elders. No special burial ceremonies exist even for elders. It is the common belief that all dead persons go to heaven instantaneously after death. Because of this ages old belief, the people are generally happy for the dead ones rather than sad.

Unlike on earth, no behavioral differences are found amongst people in the various localities. As a normal practice the vast majority of people do not reside at a fixed location. Living in a particular locality is not the habitual practice and around 90% of the adults are on the move all the time in groups of thousands. This is very similar in occurrence to the migrations of herds of animals in the African continent but in the moon, migration is an ever ongoing event that never ends. The actual reason for this habitual behavior is not known. Coming down from the distant past, the resident time at any one place is fixed at an interval of fourteen earth days. After stay at one place for fourteen days, the journey continues on to the next destination. The period of walking to the next destination also lasts another fourteen earth days thus equaling the number of days of stay at a place. As a result of this particular walking and staying pattern, most of the city centers have naturally got established at equal distances apart. The cities are approximately 150

44

miles apart, reflecting the distance that the groups can cover in fourteen days. As the moon people walk in similar fashion to how Neil Armstrong walked on the moon, walking seems to be a pretty easy and fun activity for the moon people.

Once they are in a city, the members of a group have the option of deciding on their next destination city. The adjacent cities are situated in seven radiating directions from each city. For thousands of years the groups have ritualistically dispersed in seven directions for some reason not actually known. Selecting the next city, and therefore the new direction to continue the journey are individual choices. Because of this unique ancient habitual selection of traveling along the seven directions all city centers were situated at the corners of a heptagonal interwoven spherical grid configuration. It somewhat resembled a 3D spherical beehive formation with heptagonal shaped grids, around the moon. Such shape was possible as the cities were located at different elevations. Because of the mass movement of people along the winding tunnel like pathways for thousands of years, all the pathways have eroded and evolved into extremely smooth and clean surfaces, just like pathways in anthills but at much larger scale. The vertical structures along these pathways bear very many historical records left by the ancient travelers, by way of paintings, poems, graffiti, carvings, etc. Historical ruins or anything of that nature having any archaeological value are not generally found. The terrains of the pathways are very irregular as they are naturally formed. Some places are narrow while others are wide. The elevations vary as well, with many uphill and downhill stretches. The moon people have done no alterations by way of construction to modify these natural paths. Along these pathways, at intermediate points, there are natural chambers, like niches. The moon people use these chambers as their resting places during their journeys. At some locations there are large sized chambers that connect to each other through tunnel like passageways.

By about the 6th to 8th days into their intercity traveling, each group meets others traveling in the opposite direction. When this happens they greet each other, pass gestures like "high fives", share their food, chit chat, nudge and push each other gently to have a little bit of fun and to reinforce their togetherness.

All the cities conduct ceremonial functions to welcome incoming visitors and to bid farewell to the outgoing visitors. As everybody either leaves a city or reaches a new city on a particular fixed day, these ceremonies are held at predetermined venues. As the logistics stand, this ceremonial function repeats on every fourteenth day in every city center. The day long ceremonies create good meeting opportunities for the people who come to the city from seven directions and the already resident people who will be heading to new cities in seven directions.

As a startup event in the agenda of the ceremony, all adult participants (men and women), consume a cocktail made of mushrooms. None of the adults ever miss it. The recipe of this cocktail has been coming down from the ancient days and is the same in all the cities. The moon people love it! The hallucinatory agents in the cocktail probably transport the minds of the people into a different realm and help them socialize, perform dances and enhance their inner bonding. Speculating on this further, the cocktail drink may be the core impetus driving their propensity for intercity traveling. The 'travelers' are assured of the reward of a dream making cocktail once every fourteen days at all the cities. Some people may be unconsciously addicted to this! No one took this special drink or any form of alcohol on the other days. However, it was an accepted norm also that the people who stayed permanently at one location lost the eligibility to have this drink. Without exception everyone observed this rule strictly without having to be policed by others.

The ceremonies generally included playing of games, beating of drums, singing, dancing, storytelling, dining and chit chat. The whole community actively took part in the ceremonies. The dances they performed seemed like a huge network of dance groups changing from one array to another every few seconds, following very thoughtfully choreographed rhythmic patterns. This was done very skillfully and with many flourishes. The people were in physical contact with each other during the entire dancing act. Vivid dancing patterns were accompanied by appropriate sound effects. The songs that were sung and the dances that were performed were the same at every city center of the moon where these parties were held. These have not changed over the many thousands of years past, just like the seasonal Christmas songs played on the radio every year.

On the day following the ceremony, the people who were due to leave the city commenced their new journeys. Those who arrived at a particular city got engaged in the chores that formed their site duties. Those who travel carry only the bare essential items including the food they need for the next 14 days of travel. The food parcels that they will take are prepared in advance. Personal musical instruments are one of the 'extra' items that people carried with them when traveling. As a means of avoiding monotony and making it interesting, walking patterns of the 'travelers' were of diverse, rhythmic styles and were almost always accompanied by appropriate sound effects. Some people also had their pets such as parrots, with them.

The specific aspect of "Fourteen days" travel and "Fourteen days" residence is not a hard and fast rule of any kind, but it is the practice that had come down from the past thousands of years. It might have something to do with half-moon day or the intervals of tidal waves that were experienced. The post ceremonial arrangements were so arranged that every person who reached a city understood what community functions they would need to be engaged in from the very next day. During their stay they attended to regular community work such as cooking, cleaning, farming, field work, gathering food from lakes, attending to various community based construction works, teaching children, day care work, etc. Nobody gave them directions as to what to do. But they sought out exactly what work was there to be done for the next fourteen days. These procedures have been repeatedly taking place over the past centuries and hence it is not difficult to understand how all these interrelated tasks were carried out so smoothly.

When moon people moved from one city to another, the moving group always mixed with others who had arrived there from the other six directions. At every new occasion, they always merged into new groups without seeking to stay with their original group. The mixing up of groups was a continuous process that took place at every city center. As a result of mixing into groups and splitting their journeys into seven directions at each city center, after a few years, it was always difficult to find another person from one's original group. This was not applicable at the individual level to a couple of a male and female as such couples always stayed together. By constantly moving from one area to another, the people were exposed to almost the entire vast area of their habitat during their life time and also made them have the opportunity to intermingle with the entire noon population of around 2 million persons. The birth and death rate has been almost equal over many thousands of years and as a result the population of people in the moon has attained a steady state. The average life span of moon people is over 100 earth years and this might be due to the type of food they ate, the ritualistic walking habit they perform for more than half their life time and perhaps the greatest influence might be the lives free from conflict and stress that they lead.

As people got older, they preferred to stay in areas of choice. Elders naturally settled into self-assumed roles of providing community advice. As all the people were fully independent while being strongly bonded to each other, they did not have a practice of keeping close contact with their immediate relatives or children or parents. They were firmly possessed of a true sense of brotherhood and sisterhood, and unwaveringly held with this concept in their dealings with their fellow

48

citizens. Moon people have a long established history of taking care of the elderly members of the population in a compassionate manner. They do not have special retirement communities or nursing homes or hospitals caring for elders. When any person gets sick, the others take care of him without need for a request to be made. All assistance that is needed on any matter is always available around them all the time. This is due to a unique sense of 'ownership' where all persons are considered as one's own; every child is regarded as one's own; every City Park, road, house, community center is considered as one's own. The sense of belongingness to the community and the community itself are inherent and inseparable parts of the social system.

When once a man and woman get together, their bond is maintained permanently. If a child is born, the mother stays with the baby for three months. During this time the baby is usually breast fed by the mother or sometimes by other mothers. Children including infants are brought up in the community centers mentioned before. Hence children do not develop social bonding to their parents. In fact nobody knows who their parents are. The moon people laid a very strong emphasis on educating the children and the children are kept in the community education system until they reach 16 years of age. The children learn academic subjects as well as all domestic practical work required for community activities. There are also chores that have to be carried out during non-study time. From a very early age, children are assigned specific responsibilities. The chores are selected suitably by community leaders with due regard to the age of the child. The children select their own names during the school period according to their sole independent choice. However the first part of the name carries the name of the city. For instance children from the city of "Vaaadi" would have names like Vaaadi Tukuuu, Vaaadi Bekiii, Vaaadi Zukooo, etc., - short names but pronounced with a long dragging accent. Written records of births or any other type of identification mechanism does not exist. Extremely brilliant children are encouraged to join exclusive sets of scholar community groups involved in scientific research. Inventions and knowledge resulting from engaging in such research are shared with the community elders and utilized appropriately for the benefit of the community. None of the research is geared to business oriented purposes and is all purely focused on community benefit and knowledge development. These research based institutions form a higher sector of the community schooling system but they are limited to a few cities and are not many in number.

Contrary to the pattern that existed in the past, the research facilities have been expanding rapidly in recent times. This is seen to be due to the younger generation's increasing interest in scientific adventure. Recent research findings of the moon people have permitted significant advances into many scientific discoveries following like pattern as the history of discoveries on earth. However, the elders adopt a very cautious attitude, being averse to technologies that might weaken their social structure. As they have come to be very comfortable with their prevailing lifestyle, they naturally exercise utmost care before introducing the applications of any scientific discoveries into their daily life. The network of elders was responsible for decisions on what was good or bad before changes were introduced to the community. Inexplicably, discoveries such as battery powered lights were restricted to the research laboratories as there was an attitude of ultra-conservativeness in the use of new technologies. The elders collectively believed that the people could well get along without modernity. The moon people value simplicity over comfort, convenience and leisure. Their lifestyle was based on a deliberate balance of avoiding a pleasure world while maintaining self-sufficiency. The networks of elders who have the responsibility to take decisions are not rulers of any kind. These groups actually function as groups of elders convened by specific situations to take decisions to deal with any new circumstance. The sets of decision making groups vary from day to day, from subject to subject and from city to city. Conflicts do not arise amongst any of these elders as they are all very broadminded and also have similar frames of mind. As elders in each city took appropriate decisions on communal matters pertaining to their particular city, intercity communication was not a pressing necessity. However in the instances where they had to consult the other prominent elders in adjacent cities, it took place at a very slow pace as avenues for advanced communication, such as telephones were not known in the moon.

The moon people had a unique system of beliefs. They did not know how the brain functioned just like people on earth 500 years ago and they believed in a soul. They presumed that all the memories that they remember are borne by an external soul associated with their physical body. So, they believed the soul was a separate entity from the body and that this soul could transmigrate. They identified the soul as their "Self". They did not have a concept of God, unlike the comparative situation with many religions on earth. However they firmly believed that the soul would instantly "Teleport" to a heaven immediately upon a person's death. They also believed that they would have youthful physical bodies when they took up their abode in heaven. They were convinced that heaven was an extremely beautiful place of pleasure with very many fun things to do and look around and enjoy. They believed that once they were in heaven, they would not age, fall ill, feel pain or have sorrowful feelings of any kind.

They believed that heaven was a community based place without a leader, or elders, and that it had a social structure identical to the one they enjoyed in the moon. They did not have a concept of "Hell" and probably did not have a word meaning "sin" or any word with a meaning even slightly resembling it. Words such as sin, cruelty, evil, jealousy, anger, crime, fight, aggression, war, etc., were totally unknown to the moon people.

From ancient times, through the transparent areas of the moon's crust the people of the moon had seen a beautiful planet like object in the sky. They believed that it was heaven (meaning "pleasure place" in their language)… the place that they will be born in after their death. This heaven was visible only from certain cities of the moon. The entire moon population was aware of this heaven from their school education and also from reports by people who had seen it. Like certain religious pilgrimages on earth, part of the purpose of the "moon people's continuous movement habit" was to observe this heavenly body during their lifetime. Most people had seen the heaven when they arrived at cities from which it was visible. However, it should be understood that the primary purpose of the movement habit was not to satisfy a need to see the heaven. The primary purpose of the habitual journeying was really not known. Whenever the moon people approached a place from where they could see this beautiful heaven in space for the first time, they had the background knowledge that getting to heaven was an event that would take place at the end of their lifetimes. They were therefore very excited and overwhelmed by it. However, when they actually got to look at the object which was heaven they would glare at it for long hours without blinking as it was so utterly beautiful and enjoyable to look at – like a glowing blue colored gem hanging by itself. Just looking at it gave them a sense of deep fulfillment. The city centers from where heaven could be seen had more ceremonial events and cocktail drinks than other cities. The moon people's migratory journey did not end at these cities or any other place and continued in a closed and never ending chain. Because of the continuous nature of the movement routine, none of the moon people could remember where they spent their childhood or any other place specific details of their journey. This did not matter to them because the life style at all parts of the moon was similar, routine, efficiently structured and very pleasant. The moon people had no doubt at all that at the end of their lives, they would all end up at heaven - the pleasure place. To the reader of course there is no awe associated with the object the moon people see as heaven but to the moon people it is a fundamental fact on which their whole life's purpose is pinned.

There have been prominent philosophers, artists, poets, scientists and other scholars in the moon. They have contributed a wealth of benefits to the moon community by spreading their knowledge and ideas. The old generations have kept the harmony of the moon community intact. The elders in the moon at present have been somewhat perturbed in the recent past with the present generation of children, who seek to express their reasoning as to how they wish to move forward into the future. The elders have observed trends of some individuals tending to deviate from the traditional social system and attempting to adopt different living styles. But up to now the elders have been able to address such situations and have managed to keep the traditional systems intact. Since some time now a common vision has arisen amongst many elders that an upheaval of colossal proportions could occur in their social lifestyle in the near future; not due to natural phenomena but due to idealistic inclinations of present day youth.

The Intellectuals and Research ••• ••••

Similar to primitive hunter gatherers on the earth, who observed the sun, stars and other heavenly bodies over thousands of years, the moon people have observed these objects over thousands of years. However, they had to make these observations through the limited areas of moon surface that was transparent. There are many mythical stories as well as valuable observations that the ancestors of the moon have passed on to succeeding generations. After invention of the telescope by the moon people, their knowledge of astronomy has widened, but their knowledge of the universe is very limited and cannot be compared at all to any discoveries made by our pioneering astronomers of even way back as the fifteenth century. The moon astronomers were lucky not to have religious authorities to upset them unlike what Galileo and Kepler had to face when they proclaimed their discoveries. The moon astronomers did not know about the planets in the solar system or how the planets were kept moving relative to each other by the dynamic forces between them. It is quite understandable that they did not know more about astrophysics, having had to spend their lives within a system of caves. To have an opportunity to view stars and other objects shining through clear glass like surfaces, on the roofs of their cave world was considered a great treat by the moon people, as these were rare occasions for them. However, they got opportunities to see outer space, usually several times, during their constant routine of travel from city to city. As such, most people were aware of the outside world and the fact that they were living within a system of caves.

The clarity of space objects depended on the clearness of the transparent moon surfaces. Though there were many relatively clear moon surfaces these were not at all as clear as colorless glass on earth. The varying thicknesses and the irregularities on the surfaces made the clarity of the space objects seen through the 'clear' moon surfaces relatively poor. Apart from the clear areas, there were vast areas of transparent moon surface covered by dust like material hindering outer space visibility. The moon people had no way of clearing the dust from these surfaces as these areas were beyond access to them. As a very useful practical outcome, clearing of these dust covered areas would increase sunlight penetration into the caves thus enhancing illumination and the growth of vegetation. In the recent past the moon astronomers had acquired a deeper interest in seeing more and more of the outside worlds from different parts of the moon. As a further step they explored avenues to expand their total viewing area. Sometimes nature would help to clear dust from viewing areas. This happened when solid bodies, such as asteroids or comets collided on nearby surfaces. These objects that fell at high velocities created shock waves along the surface, thus helping sometimes to dislodge dust from viewing areas. As the moon did not have an external atmosphere to burn out these objects, these collisions were more frequent on the moon than on earth. Though millions of scarred impact craters are found on the moon, meteorite impacts were very rare. Sometimes these events worked negatively as well; destroying the existing clear areas by the deposition of dust and debris, arising from collisions.

There are less than two hundred institutions that work on pure research and development in the entire moon. The locations of these institutions are spread over the moon far apart from each other. Knowledge sharing amongst these institutions does occur but at a low scale due to lack of quick communication capabilities. These research and development centers are led by very keen intellectuals dedicated to expanding their realm of understanding of specific scientific fields that they are working on. The research institutions are staffed by very intelligent children, identified when they were at the community schools. As directed by elders in the community schools, these children are encouraged to join the researchers when they become adults. But after joining these institutions over 95% of these intelligent children leave the researchers and join the common traveling society as they have been pre-programmed to do so. Millions of years of evolution of the brain have made traveling their inherent natural choice. Probably their genes are etched to stay with this social trend. However, a minority of intellectuals stay on to pursue research as a serious dedicated group.

About two hundred years ago after the invention of the telescope, the scientists in the moon realized the benefit of developing optical lenses and mirror systems further. The research over the last 200 years on this field had made progress toward developing and improving compound optical lens configurations that can concentrate light into very narrow beams. Though these light beams are not comparable to LASER beams, the moon scientists have been contemplating their use as an intercity communications medium. In fact they have installed these compound-lens systems to keep contact between research organizations separated by a distance exceeding 150 miles. Success has been achieved in sending a light beam from one institute to the other. These beams are relayed along the pathways that moon people travel on from city to city. A number of compound lens devices have been installed at many junctions to receive and direct the beam appropriately to follow the required path. The light source of the system is the material "Babaloniums" which produces light of intensity adequate for the purpose. After the scientists established the system, it was acknowledged as an enormous success and development is now in progress of a "Code Book", similar to the "Code Book" of torch telegraphy that the ancient Greeks and

Romans developed. Light signals are probably the oldest method for transmitting messages between hilltops over distances on earth. Coded messages have long been transmitted from ship to ship with lights. Moon scientists are still working on the codes to perfect the system for communication amongst the research facilities.

After the moon scientists developed electrical magnets and a subsequent discovery was made of electromagnetic waves - commonly called radio waves - they did not know what to do with their new discovery. But as things happened in the earth's history, sometimes accidents lead to discoveries. As an accidental discovery, the scientists in the moon found that when electromagnetic instruments were energized, they caused a physical disturbance of nearby dust particles. Some particles were attracted and others were repelled as is the case with static electricity. They also observed that the particles responded at substantial distances of separation, even by-passing the physical barriers between instrument and particles. This observation caused them to make more powerful units which could generate more powerful waves. The leading scientist who had invented the system directed the waves towards the moon's surface with the idea of checking the effect on the moon dust lying on the transparent area of the moon's crust. The moon dust covering thin transparent surfaces was seen to be projected up and down thus making it possible to improve visibility through the transparent surface. Though it did not yield perfect transparency of the moon's crust, this was a big success. By experimenting further on this and fine tuning the apparatus, they realized that electromagnetic waves could help them to clear the dust on top of the transparent sections of the moon's surface. After several repeated applications, some small areas achieved near complete elimination of the dust cover. Obviously this was a huge discovery for the moon people as they needed to maximize sunlight penetration into the caves and also achieve as much visibility of outer space. However, powering the equipment was a problem. The type of batteries that were being used was not adequate in capacity to power the equipment for more than a few hours.

Upon the discovery of a mechanism for removing the dust on the moon's surface, the elders of the city gave their blessings to proceed further with these experiments. The name of this particular city was "Daaadi". A scientist from the same city Daaadi was the pioneer in establishing the optical communication link mentioned earlier. The communication link was from Daaadi city to a city nearby named "Laaahi". In the city of Daaadi the ceremony that was conducted every 14 days, acquired an additional feature now. This was the demonstration of their new equipment that cleared the dust on the surface crust of the moon. The scientist who invented it demonstrated the capability of his invention to the amazement and delight of all the people. Each time they energized the instrument, a greater area at the top of the caves got cleared. Though the new cleared area was like a 20ft diameter patch, it brought more sunlight to the cave during the 14 day long daytime. They could now see more of outer space. Some people repeatedly viewed this demonstration while others did not show much interest. The scientist was able to clean an additional 6 square foot area at each occasion of demonstration. However, he had to stop the demonstration after about 80 minutes due to the inadequacy of battery power. The batteries had to be switched from one set to another during the demonstration. These batteries had to be painstakingly reconditioned and recharged before the next ceremony.

Now you can understand what was causing emanation of radio waves from the moon.

Right!

Let us see what was happening on the earth and how they were going to investigate the mysterious moon people. We have to now get back to the time when "Hi!" received the moon signal (15 minutes ago). Let's refresh our memories.

This will be interesting!

Moon and SETI-NASA Interaction   "•••" "••••"   "• = Dot"

The signal strength of the moon source as detected by "Hi" and relayed to the SETI-NASA command center had been unvarying over the first 15 minutes. The instruments on the satellite reconfirmed the fact that the signal originated from below the surface of the moon by a distance of at least 30ft. As planned, the time had arrived for the SETI-NASA team to transmit the "dot", "dot", "dot" and "dot", "dot", "dot", "dot" radio waves to the target. In an atmosphere charged with expectant hope and optimism, with all eyes and ears focused on the instrument panels, the transmission from "Hi" was initiated. The transmission was maintained for five minutes paused for two minutes and the pattern was repeated. The pauses were deliberately introduced to prompt and capture the attention of the source. Even if the source reciprocated while the "dot", "dot", "dot" signal burst was on, the instruments in the satellite were capable of detecting a direct response or a variation in the pattern or intensity of the so far steady moon signal. The electronic ears were on in continuous listening mode. Unfortunately, no indication even remotely resembling a response was detected for the next sixty seven minutes at which point the signal died away abruptly. The cessation of the signal was not unexpected, but the silence that met the signal of greeting from "Hi" was very disappointing considering all the hard work put in and the enormous expectations of the staff at the SETI-NASA command center.

However though the lack of a response from the moon's signal source was no doubt a setback, other planned tasks in the overall program were executed. The satellite "Buddy" was used by the teams in conducting a wide range of investigative activities. Buddy had cameras with extremely powerful and high resolution type telephoto capture facilities to photograph the signal source area. These cameras are of a type used in agricultural crop measurement, geological and topography mapping and similar applications. The cameras in the satellite were of the highest refinement and capability with full color and 3D capability. It could read a bill board of 30ft x 30ft size and reproduce a clear image easily even at its miles long orbiting distance. This gives an indication of the quality of pictures that could be expected. The lack of an atmosphere on the moon also contributed to the enhancement of the quality of the pictures. The pictures were taken continuously according to a planned program. From time to time the camera mode was turned on to produce 3D images and other multi-resolution pictures. Towards the latter part of the picture taking program, the schedule also included taking pictures of other proximate areas that were chosen as places of interest. These included a few craters, deep valleys and flat terrain in close proximity to the source area. A special panel of image scientists had instant access to these high resolution optical images no sooner they were received by the SETI-NASA command center for their evaluation and analysis.

This satellite also had infrared (IR) thermograph camera equipment. Infrared thermograph equipment is quite different from night vision equipment. Night vision equipment amplifies the faint night light and permits seeing in the dark. IR cameras are designed to detect the thermal energy emitted by objects and produce images depicting their temperature variations and therefore IR imaging is not affected by light intensity. High temperature objects radiate more heat than cold objects. When viewed through a thermograph camera against a cooler background on the earth, humans and other animals could easily be detected and depicted as images. The thermo graphic images that were to be taken on the signal area had its own group of experts to process and interpret the images.

From previous missions, NASA had surface maps of the entire moon with a modest degree of details of its mineral composition. However, the satellite "Buddy" was equipped with a highly technologically advanced instrument known as an infrared mineralogical mapping spectrometer able to map the mineral composition around the signal area with very great accuracy. The satellite also had the most developed subsurface sounding radar altimeter. The purpose of the subsurface sounding radar altimeter was firstly to find water. The technique was to bounce radar waves off the source area and to receive and analyze the "echoes". If there were near-surface liquid water accumulations the bouncing signal would be stronger than if the signal bounced off a hard surface. Secondly, the thickness of the dust layer that covered the source area could be determined. Thirdly, the surface materials around the signal spot could be characterized. The satellite had a purpose built set of special antennae with a span of 100ft for these purposes. Other hardware packed in the satellite had capabilities to determine the surface chemistry around the source spot, including detecting the presence of moisture, gases or any other emissions from the sub-surface. All these scientific data were to be channeled to separate experts specialized in the respective fields.

The SETI-NASA team was now preparing for their next fourteenth day signal detection and messaging routine. The action plan remained more or less the same. As regards the transmission of a LASER signal in addition to the radio signal beamed by "Hi", it would be tried out after first having the radio signal on for 35 minutes. If any feedback was obtained within these 35 minutes, the radio signals would be continued with and the LASER signal will not be beamed. There was still a lot of expectation and hope of establishing a reciprocating communication arrangement with the signal source. But some riddles yet remained!

After expert review of the photographic images and various other data based on a range of tests and measurements, the principal commanders had a more detailed understanding of the area around the signal source. The image scientists were amazed at the pictures that they saw. They confirmed that the signal location was situated in an area with a vast layer of lunar regolith that had been subjected to agglutination. This finding was supported by the scientists who were involved with the infrared mineralogical spectrometer mapping. Agglutinated lunar regolith is the translucent material mentioned earlier. Most lunar regolith material samples that the Apollo program brought back to earth between 1969 and 1972 was translucent. But the surface material in the pictures appeared to be exceptionally translucent and widespread. A major portion of this area was covered with common moon dust and debris from meteorite impacts. The 3D pictures and the sounding radar altimeter gave an assessment of the terrain and the thickness of the dust layers. Pictures zoomed on the signal spot indicated a wide patch of smooth textured transparent surface. The dust layer in this area was only a few inches deep. At some spots the smooth surface layer was very clearly exposed and looked like glass. As the pictures were mostly concentrated on the signal source area, the images that were planned to be taken on craters, deep valleys and flat terrain were not available at this stage for assessment of the surrounding areas. The infrared imaging investigations performed on the signal spot revealed temperature differences between the surface and the underground. As the surface temperature depends on the time and the sector of the moon's day, the data that was available so far was not sufficient to yield a meaningful interpretation of results. However, an observation that stood out was that the subsurface temperature at the signal source area throughout the last 12 earth days was relatively steady. It was 72˚F compared to the surface temperature fluctuation of 12˚F to 220˚F. This was quite unexpected.

From the first phase of investigations performed through the infrared mineralogical mapping spectrometer, the dust on the signal area was inferred to be silicon based with a high percentage of Iron and Nickel. These results tallied with the details NASA already had from various previous reconnaissance missions.

The preliminary results obtained through the sounding radar altimeter evinced leading evidence to conclude that the signal area had a hollow subsurface. In fact some results showed that the surface thickness above the cavity seemed to vary in a range of 4 to 25 feet. To the scientists, this was a remarkable finding because of the astounding fact that the actual source of the signal was about 30 feet below ground level. The longitudinal extent of the cavity was yet to be investigated and established. Water vapor was not found on the surface. SETI Institute and NASA were very tight lipped about these findings and none of the findings were released to the public. However, media representatives were kept happy by giving them a general version of the progress of the project.

As expected the moon signal was received on the 14th day. The satellite's "dot", "dot", "dot" and "dot", "dot", "dot", "dot" radio waves were targeted at the signal source. This time the SETI-NASA team had Buddy's imaging cameras focused at the signal spot and recorded images every half second so as to detect any activity at the spot. As on the previous occasion, the satellite did not receive any response from the signal spot. It was the same old monotonous signal with a steady stream of useless data without any variation in content. NASA anticipated some intermittent breaks or differing modulation patterns in the signal in response to their message. Regrettably, none of these anticipated responses were noticed during the first 35 minutes. The SETI-NASA team decided to adopt their game plan B; that was the fire-up of the LASER beam with the same "dot", "dot", "dot" and "dot", "dot", "dot", "dot" sequence with intermittent 2 minutes of pause. This was kept on for nearly 26 minutes, until the moon signal stopped. No response was received from the signal source during this entire period.

From the data gathered during the LASER beam transmission event, the SETI-NASA team realized that the moon's surface at the signal area exhibited the properties of glass as the LASER beams easily penetrated the surface material. This piece of evidence was another remarkable fact for the disappointed but information hungry team. The immediate question that arose in everybody's mind was whether they had detected the glass dome of an alien moon base?

This thought was not new and was a big media speculation in 1994 after the US navy sent the satellite "Clementine" to the moon to compile a complete moon map. Out of the 1.8 million images Clementine took, 170,000 images were released to the public. The rest was treated as classified. Third party groups who analyzed these pictures, claimed to have found incredibly massive artificial structures on the moon in the basin of the "Tycho" Crater. Some of these pictures had been censored later by NASA. One of the structures resembled a massive glass dome. It looked like a weaver bird's nest. This was a hot topic at that time. In 1994 a group backing the claim of existence of UFO's declared this dome as the greatest discovery in history. They said the government and military agencies knew about this for decades but were concealing it from the public. They further said that the alien moon base had been there for tens of thousands of years. Existence of such a dome was denied by the NASA scientists with facts and figures but some skeptical persons still believe the government was not disclosing the truth. However, this particular dome was on the far side of the moon at a location not anywhere close to the spot that the moon signal was emanating from.

All analysis of the images taken by Buddy on the signal spot at 30 second intervals, on the day "Hi" was in touch with the moon signal, was now complete. It revealed yet another strange fact. The dust on the surface at the signal source spot seemed to be drifting to a side. These dust movements were noticed during the time the moon signal was being beamed. This movement of dust was not apparent on any other day. Many more images were taken later to confirm that this was not happening on the other days, when Buddy was flying over the spot. The scientists were busy reasoning out why this was so. If it was due to a blowing over the moon's surface, why was it not happening on the other days? However, the instruments fitted on board Buddy did not detect any blowing at all. Atmosphere over the moon's surface was virtually non-existent but there have been NASA studies of this dust levitation effect as it had also been encountered before at many places on the moon. NASA had explanations as to why some parts of the moon demonstrated levitation of dust. These explanations suggested that the dust on the surface could levitate due to continual bombardment of high energy radiation from the sun in the forms of UV, X-rays, and solar wind plasma, combined with the magnetosphere. But such an explanation would not apply to the signal spot, because the movement of dust was seen only when the moon signal was present. So, the reason for the dust movement was still a mystery, unless it could be totally attributed to the moon signal.

One of the priority tasks planned for "Buddy" at the next encounter with the signal, was to confirm the dust movement taking place once more. The question of whether the moon signal had anything to do with the dust movement arose. NASA also had scientists who researched on dust removal techniques for the previous moon missions. During the Apollo missions a dust removal technology was developed using electrostatic and di-electrophoretic forces to prevent accumulation of dust on solar panels. Scientists who continued their research on this subject were consulted to ascertain whether the radio wave phenomenon could be correlated to dust movement on the moon's surface. They seemed to think that it was highly probable but had their reservations due to lack of specific technical data on the signal.

In a desperate attempt to prompt the source to respond, instead of waiting another 14 days to capture the signal, The SETI-NASA team decided to continue the "dot", "dot", "dot" and "dot", "dot", "dot", "dot" sequence of radio waves and LASER beam signal to operate in parallel and continuously in alternating 'on' and pause mode.

Response from the Moon City Daaadi ••• ••••

As explained in the previous chapter, the moon signal had become one of the events of the 14th day celebration function. It was introduced merely to demonstrate the dust clearing ability that had so very recently been developed. This was being carried out only in the city named "Daaadi" and was performed by a scientist named Daaadi Dooda, who had invented this ingenious radio wave generating equipment. Other cities did not have this capability. Daaadi City had pioneered many scientific innovations in the past as well. Dooda was an exceptionally brilliant person. When he was a teenager the elders advised him to go into research as he was recognized as an extraordinarily intelligent teenager. He followed their advice but a few years later he could not resist the temptation to join the others in the traveling routine which he continued in for five years. During this time he had been to areas where the heaven could be seen. Like the others, he was fascinated by the heaven and its image got firmly etched in his memory. However, it might have been his fate as people say, that when he happened to came back to Daaadi through sheer random occurrence he had an urge to go back to continue the research he had started on before leaving Daaadi for the first time. All this took place 45 years ago.

Dooda had been engaged in the dust removing demonstration for some time now, while at the same time using each occasion to optimize performance of the equipment. Further research had been on-going in this field as the elders liked the benefits that the surface dust removal brought to the city as a major section of it was blessed with a transparent glass-like roof surface. However, quite unexpectedly a new event took place. On the last occasion when Dooda performed his demonstration, a narrow beam of very bright red light penetrated into the cave. All the people who participated in the ceremony saw this light beam streaming into the caves in intermittent bursts. The intensity of the incoming light ray virtually blinded them momentarily. Neither the moon people nor the moon scientist could understand what was

65

happening or think of a cause. The moon people who participated in the ceremony were amazed by the sight of such a bright ray of light as never ever seen by them before. They naturally assumed that the red light was part of the demonstration and gave full credit to their scientist Dooda. As nothing outside their expectations had occurred, these moon people continued their journeys on the next day. They would probably have forgotten all that they saw by now as the ordinary folk in the moon dwelt on their immediate impressions only very briefly and then moved on!

Though he had not come across the red light beam in any of his earlier demonstrations, the moon scientist Dooda thought that his instrument might have created the red light beam due to some unknown cause. However, the next day Dooda found that the red beam of light had not ceased its continuous pulsating glow. He also observed that the light beam extended above the cave's roof top as he could see the unbroken red line through the clear moon surface leading backwards into pitch dark outer space. He immediately realized it had a very distant source and also noticed that the beam seemed to have some kind of message as there appeared to be a deliberate pattern in the "dot", "dot", "dot" and "dot", "dot", "dot", "dot" sequence. Dooda who had developed the radio wave equipment was an individual of a high order of above average intelligence and he felt strongly that he should reciprocate the color beam signal in some manner, perhaps using a light source as well.

He consulted the elders in the city. The city elders with their enormous respect to Dooda did not object to Dooda's pursuing his line of thought. Dooda already had a plan in his mind. He needed the support of a fellow scientist named Daaadi Loola who had developed the compound optical lens configuration and pioneered the establishment of the light link between the two cities "Daaadi" and "Laaahi" mentioned earlier. Loola who was an expert on light beams was from the same city of Daaadi and did his research at the same research facility as Dooda. Readers would probably have guessed that he was from the same city based on the first part of his name. Dooda and Loola had known each other over a very long time. Loola saw the LASER beam when Dooda took him to the cave where the radio wave generator was installed. He was fascinated by the fact that the beams of light developed by him for communication purposes were very much like the LASER beam.

Loola realized that the red light was harmless. Of course Loola assessed this fact cautiously and finally felt confident to touch the LASAR beams several times. Dooda also checked it out himself on the assurance given by Loola that the red beam was harmless.

The red light beaming into Daaadi city had by now been observed over the past two days. It was visible every half an hour as regular "dot", "dot", "dot" spurts as programmed by the SETI-NASA team.

Dooda suggested that Loola help him to use his latest compound optical lens configuration to direct his light beam towards the signal source of the red light. Loola agreed and made arrangements to get his instruments relocated to the same place as where Dooda performed his dust removing demonstration. The light source of Loola's compound optical unit was a medium sized Babaloniums crystal and the beam it produced was very similar in appearance to a LASER beam.

After the head of the compound optical unit was painstakingly and precisely directed towards the best assessment of theirs of the point from which the red light beam seemed to be originate, Loola took off the cover of the lens. Dooda and Loola were now, for the very first time in their lives, seeing their Babaloniums light beam, beaming through and beyond the glassy cave hood and disappearing into black space. As they never had cause before to direct the light towards outer space, theirs was a unique observation. The pale blue colored light was visible as a single beam to a very great distance beyond the moon's surface. Dooda and Loola were ecstatic. They made further adjustments to align their light beam parallel to the LASER beam. Unlike the LASER beam the

Babaloniums light beam did not issue as an extremely narrow beam but became less intense and diffused with distance as it progressed outwards. Dooda felt that it would be appropriate and important to also arrange for the light signal to pulsate in a "dot", "dot", "dot" format. Loola advised Dooda to use the lens cover to create the effect manually. He did as best as he could to replicate the LASER signal pattern. Dooda and Loola were not sure what they should do beyond this or what to expect thereafter. They merely repeated their pulsating beam routine over a considerable period and waited, gazing at the LASER beam.

The sensitive eyes and ears of the satellite "Hi" did not take long to figure out that some very significant change had taken place at the moon's signal source spot. As soon as the Babaloniums light signal was projected to outer space, the satellite detected the faint light signal and immediately relayed the visual data to the ground station. The SETI-NASA team could not immediately comprehend the implications of this new development, especially because this happed 2 days after the usual 14 day signal. But after about twenty minutes the team decided to concentrate on the fact that this was what they had been waiting for - "A response from the source". This was the biggest "Aha!" moment for the scientists. They delayed no longer. The satellite was commanded to change the "dot", "dot", "dot" signal to a different one. A new sequence of "dot", "dot" followed by a 30 sec. pause was implemented.

For Dooda and Loola almost 30 minutes had passed after they sent out their last signal. They were not inclined to wait much longer and decided to get back to their normal routines. However almost as if fate had willed it, SETI-NASA's new "dot", "dot" signal arrived just in time to catch their attention. Dooda and Loola realized that the message was different. That was an "Aha!" moment for both of them too. They reacted immediately and sent back a "dot", "dot" signal. The SETI-NASA team was thrilled to have got such an immediate response. This time the SETI-NASA team changed their signal to five "dots". Dooda and Loola reciprocated with five "dots". This exchange of communication signals went on and on. As a further variation, the SETI-NASA team deliberately stopped their signal. When this happened, Dooda and Loola waited for some time with puzzled looks on their faces. They however seemed to instinctively understand how they might be able to respond to break the silence and they initiated a seven "dot" signal. The SETI-NASA team reciprocated with a seven "dot" signal. SETI-NASA went into "dots" and "dash" signal combinations. To their great joy, the moon source reciprocated in matching fashion.

By now, it was certain that the moon source was active and live. "What will this say to the entire world?" – This question kept resonating in the minds of all the people who were working on the signal. The SETI-NASA team realized that the last signal was a good indication that they would be able to lead this exercise into a meaningful dialogue. The SETI-NASA team as well as Dooda and Loola were keen on prolonging this communications event and it went on many long hours. However, though the SETI-NASA team tried out various measures to upgrade the interaction into a meaningful exchange of information they failed to elevate it beyond a mere reciprocation of each other's signals. How could the interaction be developed at least to the level of exchanging basic ideas? This was the biggest question. Although very many hours were spent by a panel of experts on this subject at the planning stages, so far none of their ideas and attempts led to any useful outcome. This was the major deadlock that the SETI-NASA team was at.

The SETI-NASA team knew that they were dealing with a signal source in the moon. They realized that this discovery overshadowed all the discoveries man had ever made. This event would stand among the most momentous of events in the history of mankind. The SETI-NASA team was a highly dedicated, motivated and also now a very apprehensive group of individuals. In contrast Dooda and Loola, who unlike the SETI team, were not researchers looking for extraterrestrial intelligence, were surprised and excited as well but not very concerned as to who or what they were dealing with.

You are lucky. You know what is happening at both ends!

Releasing the News to the Public ••• ••••

The questions that the SETI-NASA team faced now were multifaceted. Far more complex and wide ranging than before! Who was behind the responding signals? Could there be living beings under the moon's surface? What would they look like? Could these light beams have been generated by a base established and populated by aliens? Or could this be an alien instrument base controlled remotely from some other unknown site in the universe? When would they be able to gain further knowledge on this? How were they to proceed further? What steps would be required to obtain clearance from the government to release this information? How could the SETI-NASA team be keep control on what facts were to be made known?

It had been an uncontested assumption that any alien life forms in the universe that might try to contact earth would be superior to humans both physically and in intellect. The finding of extraterrestrial life outside our planet would have a big impact on the philosophical and sociological structure of human beings. It would send a massive distress signal to our human psyches, pointedly challenging the assumption that we are the most advanced life form in the universe. The news might also trigger wide spread panic.

Some decades ago, a number of intellectuals brought these facts and issues to the attention of the SETI Institute to prepare them for such eventualities. The SETI Institute carefully perused and considered these ideas and evolved pre-defined policies, protocols and guide lines defining how the information should be disclosed to the domestic and international public, concerning the existence of or contact with extraterrestrial life forms. As the release of information was a huge responsibility on the ruling government, the SETI Institute sought the participation of regulatory bodies and jointly finalized the format and content of all policies, protocols and guidelines. It is a well-known fact that in the nineteen sixties, the Moon Treaty that was drawn up, proclaimed the obligation to disclose any organics found on the moon or elsewhere. At the time these drafts were conceived, the preparatory works seemed to have been based on possibly farfetched expectations and predictions of an alien encounter. But, taking the whole world community by surprise the time arrived when these protocols and policies had to be actually implemented.

Officials of SETI Institute and NASA met with Federal government officials to discuss the issue of the release of information, as they had clear evidence that an interactive exchange had occurred with the moon signal source. As this was an event of extraordinary significance and was also one without precedent; the decision making process as regards the specific content and scope of information to be released was a complicated issue and constituted a bureaucratic nightmare.

The media grew suspicious and formed the view that secretive exchange were taking place between SETI Institute, NASA and governmental officials, as their discussions had already gone on into a full second day. The government officials were yet not decided whether or not to treat all the information as classified. If it were to be treated as classified, security clearance was needed on the specific information to be released to the public. If not they could treat all the information as unclassified and permit it to be broadcast in the public domain, as had been done in the past. Due to the vast public interest in the project, the US government was under extreme pressure to release a news bulletin without much further delay. Some groups of governmental advisors held the view that the news might create panic locally and internationally. The more generally held view however, was that the news would definitely have short term unsettling effects but that these would fade out and not be operative in the medium or long term. The main short term effect would be panic among some sections of the people due to disturbances to their psyche by the discovery of extra-terrestrial intelligence. However, whether the news was released or not, media responses and hype could cause havoc amongst the general public and bring to bear disruptive and devastating consequences which would have to be handled by the federal, state and local government units. Separately also, complications could be caused by political maneuvering by various groups seeking advantages in the context of the turmoil created.

Even though the United States had in place the Freedom of Information Act, in actual fact, the government had retained many past documents connected with space exploration, under classified status. The silence of a few days led to enormous pressure being exerted by the media to release whatever findings were available at the time. The US government could not continue their silence and had to decide one way or another. A bold decision by the President of the United States resulted in all agencies being authorized to release information without reservation. There was a mood of optimism amongst most officials that any negative effects would recede very quickly.

NASA began to release all their findings in the various media formats including still pictures and videos. Within a few minutes, their website crashed due to a severe overload of internet traffic but this problem was put right within the day. Unlike many governmental documents that had been released online, the NASA documents did not have blacked out parts. The curiosity of the world population was fed with news freely and accurately.

The groups that claimed the existence of UFOs declared this to be the day they had been waiting for, though nobody in the group was quite sure exactly what the moon signal source would turn out to be.

In double quick time the news reached all corners of the globe. There was a great diversity of responses through various public media. Some were very spontaneous and joyous while others were urging utmost caution. The range of responses varied with two near equal large segments one extremely positive and other extremely negative while neutral groups were small in number. Everybody was trying to make sense of the event, projecting their own interpretations as to what or who was behind the mysterious response from the moon.

Those who were inclined to view the event positively felt the aliens or the mysterious source to be very advanced and of compassionate nature. Terms of description such as "Godly figures" were mentioned along with the suggestion that one day they would get in touch with the earth and bestow it with wisdom, kindness and comfort. However those who were apprehensive imagined that the aliens would be fearsome, ruthless warriors who might one day destroy the earth. The neutral groups were not interested in speculating on what the aliens might be like. They did not project their fears or premonitions and decided to stay with the basic fact only that there was a single indication of a signal from the moon in response to the signal from our satellite "Hi" in moon orbit.

Many scholarly presentations and articles on TV, the newspapers and in accredited science magazines appeared commenting on the pros and cons of communicating with aliens and eventually meeting them. Some of the optimistic scholars spelled out the benefits that would result from contact with the aliens as well as the potential issues that would be thrown up by encountering them physically. They pointed to the fact that the aliens might be thousands of years ahead of us and could help us in improving on food production technology & nutritional inputs, medicine & health care and possibly many more areas; Sociological benefits such as elimination of ill will, development of unity and achieving of harmonious living; Solving the riddle of the origin of life; Acquiring information on other known worlds and civilizations and belief systems; Understanding their perspectives on our ultimate destination, belief systems, self, secular movements for altruistic service; and solve the fundamental mysteries of the universe as they could have interacted also with other civilizations in the universe. The Aliens could also assist us in intergalactic missions and provide know how to organizations such as NASA to enable them to undertake such missions. NASA could even tap into the vast bank of knowledge that the aliens have gathered over ages. It was hardly possible to limit the range of avenues that might open up ... Even hard headed scientists found their minds swimming in all manner of wishful thoughts.

Some religious leaders were deeply shaken by the news. They were very restrained in making comments or stating their opinions as they wished to avoid running the risk of creating controversy within their doctrines. Most religious practices are based on relatively rigid or inflexible belief systems and strong group loyalties. Science had not helped most belief systems in the past. To safeguard their beliefs against threats that might arise from this encounter, the clergy united and armed themselves with their own interpretations. There was actually nothing new from their point of view. They had been able to overcome such situations in past centuries when conflicting scientific discoveries were encountered. The last thing they wanted however was for the aliens to force on the earth community another religion in the midst of the technological and culture shock that the discovery of their existence had already created.

The "Extreme Negatives", those who were badly perturbed by the news had a lot to say. Their main request was "do not disturb the hornets' nest". Their fear and expectation of adverse consequences from the alien encounter were drastically opposite to the positive benefits enumerated by the "Extreme Positives". Some of this negativity could possibly be attributed to a few causes. These could be the events shown in movies on aliens that they have seen, reflection on how powerless groups have been treated by powerful ones in the past centuries, and also partly due to the influence of their religious and other beliefs.

Some arguments of the "Negatives" were very logical and worth being considered seriously. They were of opinion that the signal source should not be contacted any further without knowing absolutely what or who was behind it. Hasty action could result in utterly irreversible disaster. "Time is on our side!" they thought. Another valid major issue was what justification there was for the USA or some group in USA to take a decision on behalf of the whole world, as an encounter with aliens would without doubt have a serious impact on the entire world and not USA alone. What type of safeguard could USA provide to the other countries if the whole episode turned out to be a catastrophe? The

"Negatives" asserted that The United Nations Organization should step in and suspend all further action by the SETI-NASA team until world consensus was reached.

The SETI-NASA team was still in touch with the moon signal source by way of the light/LASER signal combination. By this time the SETI-NASA team had come to realize that there was no possibility as yet to engage in meaningful radio communication.

You know why it is? Yes of course! -- But not the SETI-NASA team!

However, use of the radio signal would be considered again in the future as it was a better way of communicating. This did not occur to Dooda and Loola as they were fascinated by the exchange of light signals. Even if they had realized it, they were ignorant of how to manipulate a radio signal effectively. They could only transmit but even so, they did not know this fact as they thought of their transmitter as a device to remove dust on the roof of their caves.

The days up to the next 14th day transmission seemed to pass quicker than before. As usual the SETI-NASA team received the radio signal. The movement of dust was observed and it was confirmed that the radio signal correlated directly to the movement of dust. After several weeks of study, the SETI-NASA team concluded that if there were living beings directly sending out these signals, they could not be more technologically advanced than mankind on the earth. If however the signals were operated remotely then the aliens responsible for the remote operations could be highly advanced. Such advanced aliens could already know our language through surreptitious gathering of information from us. If so, they themselves would be capable of compiling a language that the SETI-NASA team could understand. But nothing of this sort had happened so far so that it would be reasonable to think that technologically advanced aliens were not involved.

The signal exchanges so far have been relatively passive and uninformative. The SETI-NASA team was exerting themselves to the utmost to introduce a meaningful code into their LASER communication to establish a dialog. But it proved to be more difficult than expected. People have had a limited amount of success in communicating with animals without the use of words. Interacting with Dolphins is a good example. But in the successful instances sign language has had to be used. Loola already had experience in coding light signals to deliver messages between the moon cities of Daaadi and Laaahi. But as those codes were based on the language used by the moon people, his experience did not help either.

Could the light signal sequences be pursued further to develop a dialog with the remote source? It seemed like an impossible task. However, Loola who had experience in this field suggested to Dooda that they transmit three "dots", a small pause, two more "dots" and then five "dots" after a big pause to indicate that it was the value resulting from addition of the previous three and two "dots". Dooda did as Loola suggested. This sequence was repeated a few times. The SETI-NASA team understood the message. Immediately the SETI-NASA team sent similar math questions to Dooda to answer. They answered it correctly. This confirmed that Dooda's original signal was a math question. They understood each other's math questions correctly and reciprocated in the sending of answers. This was a new development that was initiated by the moon people. These innovations strengthened interactions to a much greater extent but the arithmetical question and answer sessions did nothing to elevate the significance of the exchange of information. What was now required was to move to a higher step at least to be able to code in a simple questions such as "What is your name?"; Mere continuation of the exchanges so far would take them only to an increased state of frustration.

It was noticed that there were instances where the light signal from the moon did not respond to the satellite signal. The SETI-NASA team was of the view that such cases coincided with periods of resting of the signal source as the intervals were of a repetitive nature. These observations led to some progress in communications. The SETI-NASA team introduced a wakeup call to the moon source with a long "dash" signal. They named it the "hello" signal and both parties understood it very well. Progressing further, they established that a signal with 3 "dashes" denoted "Bye! Bye!" and it was beamed at the end of a long communications session. However, as time passed both parties began to see that they were not making any further progress nor did they have any idea as to what more they could do.

The satellite could see the moon's light signal better when the signal spot was in the night phase of the alternating 14 earth day cycle of moon's day and moon's night. Dooda and Loola too realized this as they could clearly see their light signal penetrating the moon's surface when their city was in the night phase. As the days passed, the SETI-NASA team as well as Dooda and Loola preferred to engage in their signals exchange, during the night phase in their city. For Dooda it meant being at work for 14 continuous earth days.

The SETI-NASA team realized that their decision on inclusion of the LASER equipment in the satellite "Hi" had given by far the highest return on investment as it proved to be "the vital unit" that really established the communication link with the source and confirmed with data that the signal originated from a source 30 ft. below the moon's surface.

The jubilant feeling the SETI-NASA team enjoyed a few months ago at establishing the communications link, had been gradually fading away and was on the verge of vanishing. The inability to develop even a very basic language to have a meaningful simple dialogue with the moon source was very frustrating to the SETI-NASA team members. It was felt that the time had come to take stock of the achievements so far and plan future strategies. At the back of their minds they were happy that the Phase 1 satellite program had exceeded its targets and in fact was a huge success though the very success was a cause for frustration due to the inability to expand the communications link that was established. Both "Hi!" and "Buddy" had fulfilled their purposes fully up to and beyond the expectations of all involved. It had covered the groundwork to prepare for Phase 2 of the project. Grateful thanks "Hi! and Buddy" was the appropriate quote of the day!

It is time to implement Phase 2 and unravel the mystery of "the reply from the moon".

Phase 2 - Robotic Approach ••• ••••

The original plan for Phase 2 was to send a probe like the Mars Rover, to scout around the location of the signal source and make close-up examinations by utilizing remote sensors. The probe was to have a high powered drill which could drill to 30 feet below the moon's surface coupled with ultra-sonic instruments to study sub-surface conditions of the moon. The SETI-NASA team was now in a position to review their plan to make the robotic probe to carry out a range of tasks. They also saw that their Phase 3 plan for a manned mission within a few years would be required to be moved on to the fast track. The implications of the exchanges that had taken place up to now very compellingly indicated a need to undertake such a mission.

Could there be beings living under the outer surface of the moon? Or was the moon merely an alien base with only monitoring instruments? These were the two main alternative possibilities considered amongst a host of questions that the SETI-NASA team had to ponder over.

The interactive relationship that was established with the moon signal source gave an added impetus to efforts to expedite Phase 2 of the project. Due to the diligence, dedication and commitment of the core group of scientists who designed the Mars probes, "Spirit" and "Opportunity" and then moved on to Phase 2 of the moon project, the design part of the works had already advanced ahead of schedule. The scientists visualized many exciting findings being made through the exploratory activities of the probe that they would put together.

Phase 1 findings caused the team's focus to almost exclusively concentrate on the moon's underground. The evidence of the moon's signal source being 30 ft. below the surface and also the 'reply' light signal beamed from below ground level suggested the existence of a hollow sub-grade immediately above the level of the signal source. Further investigation confirmed that the hollow section in the area extend over a wide expanse. The surface or in effect the 'roof' thickness of the cavity ranged from 5ft to 25ft when measured around the immediate vicinity of the signal source but exceeded even 50 feet at points at a considerable distance away from the signal source. The obvious essential step to investigate into this mystery was drilling into the cave and looking into and around the interior of the cavity with electronic eyes. The SETI-NASA team knew that they would have to drill at least 5 ft to penetrate into the cave if they worked through the part where the roof of the cavity was thinnest. As a measure of prudence, the goal for drilling depth was made 20ft to provide a margin against adverse circumstances that might be encountered at the spot where the probe would actually do the drilling. On penetrating into the cave cavity it was planned to investigate the interior by use of remote sensing equipment, including various arrays of cameras such as infrared and thermal imaging devices. The SETI-NASA team was confident that the basic investigations would lead to a positive answer to the question of whether the source was manipulated by intelligent beings living on the moon, or whether it was some sort of instrument base, remotely controlled by intelligent aliens at some other location in the universe. Apart from catering to the basic requirements, the other features that were necessary to be incorporated into the Phase 2 scope of works were taken up for review in brain storming sessions.

The SETI-NASA team knew they had to be cautious and ensure that drilling and probing activities would create the least possible disturbance to any aspect of the environment around the signal source. If there were living beings in the caves, intrusive action could easily upset them and drive them away thus jeopardizing all the progress achieved. Drilling could also lead to damage to the moon's signal generating equipment. Because of this concern the very first part of the plan was to reconnoiter the area surrounding the signal spot and understand it fully before attempting drilling. Drilling at a predefined spot on the moon's surface could be achieved by just landing a probe on the exact spot without having to have a rover in the project. The moon rover idea was pursued specifically to be able to support carrying out of investigations of the surrounding area before deciding on an exact location at which to commence drilling.

If the SETI-NASA team eventually found living beings in the cave, how should the instruments interact with them? Should the SETI-NASA team indicate from which planet the instruments came? Should we prepare a memento like the gold plated disc that was placed in the Pioneer 10 space craft to be picked up by an alien discoverer? How could the instruments carried for investigational tasks be made alien-friendly? Would living beings encountering them react with hostility and destroy all the invaluable instruments that were entered into the caves? If on the other hand the cave were an aliens' signal base, what would be the appropriate course of action to be followed by us? The SETI-NASA team assigned questions and aspects of this nature to special sub-teams to derive appropriate answers and prepare action guidelines.

During the time that all these developments were taking place, several worldwide agencies were working on designing of lunar surface robots. This did not follow from the moon signal episode but resulted from the international competition promoted by the X-prize Foundation. The challenge set for the Google Lunar X-prize was development of a low cost method for robotic space exploration. To win $30 million in prize money, a robot had to be developed that could be placed on the moon's surface to explore up to a 1/3 mile radius and transmit videos back to earth. Carnegie Mellon University's school of computer science was one of the agencies eyeing the X-prize. They already had a lunar rover called "Scarab" that they had designed by this time. Though it had drilling capabilities, it was almost a toy compared to the type of unit that would suit Phase 2 exploration work. The SETI-NASA team and their moon project were becoming very popular because of their openness and the interesting presentations on the progress achieved broadcast from time to time through the media. Most of the institutions doing research and development work on the X-prize competition extended their voluntary assistance to SETI-NASA teams whenever requested. Team members met these competitors on several occasions to interact with their novel ideas.

To design a mechanism capable of drilling 20 ft. into the moon's surface based on commands originated from earth was quite a big challenge. The difficulty was less related to the remoteness and more related to the many limitations applicable to drilling on the moon. Surface drilling on the moon was going to be very difficult whether percussion drilling or straight drilling was employed. As the moon had a low gravity equivalent to 1/6 of the earth's, the drilling platform's weight was much lower on the moon than it would have been on earth. But the ability to penetrate was dependent on the total downward force that the drill could exert. Every extra ounce of cargo increased project costs tremendously. As drilling through the lunar regolith was the all-important and essential task of the entire Phase 2 sector of the project, the drill had to be designed to meet the main criterion of having the highest possible reliability while keeping within strict mass, volume and power limits. The minimum diameter of drill hole that could permit the probes and accessories to be inserted was no less than 4 inches. This was another challenge as the drill would have to be equipped with a considerably high powered drill to be able to make a 4 inch diameter penetration.

The SETI-NASA team realized that the existing satellite "Hi!" was quite adequately equipped to cater to the new robotic probe's navigational and operational needs. They were also planning to continue to use the satellite "GBU" as it was merely a transponder. Buddy was decommissioned from all activity, deactivated and made to crash on the near side of the moon adding more space junk on the moon surface.

This reduced some of the routine duties of "Hi!" and "GBU". Additional functional software programs were required for "Hi!" to work in conjunction with the robotic probe on tasks planned for Phase 2. Uploading this software and assigning the new tasks to "Hi!" was easy. However "Hi!" would not be relieved from its current duties and in fact would continue during the entire Phase 2 planned exploratory works to keep the present interaction intact and ongoing with the signal source. The SETI-NASA team thought that by doing so, they could ascertain and neutralize any negative consequences or disturbance caused by their drilling down through the surface of the moon. However, the main thinking in continuing with "Hi!" was to be able to preserve the existing 'dialogue' with the signal source during the entirety of phase 2 activities.

When the probe was finally designed it had the following features.

- A "Lander"; with a bottom structure similar in shape to the Russian Luna 20 that landed on the moon, drilled into the lunar soil and brought back samples to earth.

- The Lander had hydrazine propellant operated thrust rockets for rocket assisted landing and controlled hovering over the moon surface to carry out planned operations.

- The drill rig was mounted on the Lander.

- The drill was designed to be operated by nitrogen gas driven motors. Liquid nitrogen cylinders were packed into the base of the Lander. The added weight from the gas cylinders would help as ballast for the rig for initial drilling stability.

- The communications equipment necessary to relay commands to the rover and relay information back and forth to and from satellite "Hi!" that was linked to the earth station through "GBU".

- A rover was mounted on the Lander. The rover could egress for field works and return to its 'nest' on the Lander as commanded by ground control. The egress ramp was extendable as required and had automatic angle adjusters.

- The rover was very similar to the Mars Rovers ("Spirit" and "Opportunity") and had six wheels mounted on a rocker-bogie suspension system for negotiation on rough terrain.

- A radioisotope energy generator powered the rover while the Lander had solar arrays as well as radioisotope thermoelectric generators for electric power.

- A total of 8 cameras were mounted on one assembly on the rover which could record and transmit high definition pictures, 3D pictures, panoramic views, and infrared pictures. There was also equipment for thermo graphic imaging.

- The telescopic rod of the drill rig was designed to carry cameras and other sensory instruments into the cave once access to the cavity was established. These were detachable attachments with wireless connection to the main console of the Lander. The telescopic rod protruding into the cave could be extended up to 40ft and also rotated a full 360°.

- Apart from these, various other instruments that were required for supplementary functions were also fitted on the Lander as well as the rover.

- No high caliber rock or soil testing plans were included.

While the SETI-NASA team were making their final plans to launch the work horse probes (named "Master" the Lander and "Collie" the rover), the mainstream media was very busy, both keeping the public up to date on project progress and also monitoring and presenting public reactions and responses. The "Negatives" discouraged the project even more strongly. Mass protests, in the form of public demonstrations were seen in many states in USA and many cities in several countries demanding that the project be stopped. The rulers of some countries were pressurized by anti-project groups to request the President of the United States to stop the project and also to take up the matter with the UN. There were many incidents around the world as a result of these protests that had in some instances been suppressed aggressively. The mainstream media gave wide coverage to these events. Some of the protests were directly aimed at the United States rather than at any specific organization or group, in an attempt to politicize the matter. However the overwhelming world voice was one of support for the project and the protesters were in the main ignored.

After NASA's moon exploration missions in the early 1970s, the present project was projected as the next moon exploration program that most captured the public imagination. People seemed to be totally unconcerned about the project cost and no consideration of cost savings was brought up in discussions. This fact seemed to demonstrate that people were very willing to fund prohibitive sums on a project that would provide answers to deeply embedded and fundamental issues of human curiosity. Countries such as Japan, China and Russia who had long term goals in establishing lunar bases were watching impatiently and with great interest. So were many religious leaders, space enthusiasts and science oriented people.

Amidst protests, cheers, greetings, encouragement and objections the launching of Master and Collie took place as planned and without a hitch. Collie was ensconced in Master's belly to form a single unit with it; Master was programmed to land on the moon with the assistance of descending rockets. "Hi!" with additional capabilities would remain stationed in Luna-stationary orbit above the signal spot to relay commands from ground control to Master. NASA was able to install both Master and Collie in a single launch rocket. The module would first make communication links with "Hi!" in Luna-stationary orbit and thereafter Master with Collie on board would make a soft landing close to the signal source spot. Since no humans would land on the moon it was left to the robotics to address all the tasks including acting as ambassador from earth if any living beings were encountered on the moon. The Media had free access to most of the information on the project from NASA without restraint. This would also include some of the video streams that were planned to be received from the mission's probes landed on the moon.

Master& Collie on the Moon ••• ••••

After four and a half days of journeying and half a day in orbit around the moon, the radio links between NASA command center, GBU, Hi! and Master were checked and confirmed to be fully operational, "Hi!" and the "Master & Collie" combined unit were then brought to the ready to seek out their separate assigned destinations. NASA then commenced the countdown for Mater's descent under coordination through Hi!

The target was to land Master 500ft away from the signal source spot on the moon. A specific landing place had been selected during the planning sessions after considering many influencing factors. The surface thickness of the cave in this area was well over 40 feet and would insulate the signal spot from any disturbance due to impact. There were also no jagged projections on the rocks around the chosen landing location as previously recorded data had shown.

On the 5th day after the launch, as planned, NASA was able to land Master almost at the exact spot that they had chosen. Master provided undistorted and high resolution video coverage while Hi! was beaming commanding signals accurately to Master to ensure a precise landing. The project teams were thrilled at concluding the landing successfully. NASA discovered that maneuvering for landing on the moon was very much simpler than commanding the probes on Mars due to the very much greater proximity to the moon. Within six hours of landing, NASA had checked and found that all the instruments in Master and Collie were working perfectly. However, Collie had to leave the belly of Master to be able to verify whether its cameras and other test equipment on it were fully functional. The pictures sent to ground control indicated that Master was on flat terrain and that egress of Collie from Master would not be a problem. Commands were issued to Master to activate the ramp to permit Collie to get down and on to the moon's surface. Commands were next given to Collie to drive down the ramp. As commanded by NASA, Collie was able to clamber out of the ramp and on to the moon's surface and drive 20ft away from Master without encountering any problems. Like a playful puppy, Collie turned round 180 degrees as if it were trying to look at what Master was doing. It was a possibility that someone in the SETI-NASA team was deliberately behind this move to emulate a playful act.

These procedures took place at daytime on the far side of the moon and the signal spot area had a moderate temperature. In order to minimize any potential disturbance to the signal source, all these procedures were scheduled to be carried out when the moon signal was in the rest mode. After checking, rechecking and confirming that all instruments on Collie were operational, Collie was ready to get on with its tasks. The very first instructions were to drive Collie to various places located about 100ft from the signal spot and take high definition pictures. The SETI-NASA team ensured that the pictures were taken while the moon signal was not in operation. Collie carried out all the commands sent from earth via GBU, Hi! and Master, and took detailed photos while moving to several specific locations around the signal spot as directed by ground control. The navigational video streams sent to earth by Collie were very helpful for NASA to command Collie where to stop for picture taking.

The LASER beams were clearly seen in the pictures taken by Collie thus confirming that Collie had indeed arrived at the right area. After examining the pictures the SETI-NASA team understood that the major part of the surface in this area was comprised of material of varying degrees of translucency. The moon's surface at the signal spot was clear and glass-like. At this spot, the surface was also clear of dust over an area roughly 30ft in radius. This clear area was not actually circular but of somewhat irregular shape. The area beyond this clear section was mostly covered with moon dust but yet there were some patches here and there without the moon dust. The dustless patches seemed to have a very smooth textured and bottle glass like appearance with colors varying from brown to green. The previous imaging exercises had more or less established that the entire area was flat terrain devoid of large boulders. Thus it was quite tempting for the SETI-NASA team to send Collie over the signal spot to take pictures of the scene directly underground. However, they restrained themselves as such an act could be interpreted as an invasive move.

The second task assigned to Collie was to use its ground penetrating radar equipment to map a wide expanse around the signal spot to obtain a plot of the surface thickness variations over the cave. This was planned to be done in a 10ft x 10ft grid pattern and the primary purpose was to find an appropriate place for drilling into the cave. Collie was instructed to proceed with this work as the next task. The SETI-NASA team also ensured that Collie would always stay some distance away from the signal spot. The mapping exercise was estimated to need around 24 hours to complete the survey of an area of 300ft x 300ft. At every grid node Collie was also assigned to perform a series of non-destructive tests such as GPR (Ground Penetrating Radar) at various frequencies to profile the substrate. All readings taken by Collie were instantly relayed to NASA, through the link connecting Master, Hi! and GBU.

Using the GPR data, computers at NASA automatically produced 3D underground images. The SETI-NASA scientists could look at the data as a complete 3D block or also as horizontally or vertically sliced sections. Some of the data seemed to point to the presence of liquids deep under, but it was not a very strong indication. The SETI-NASA team was greatly surprised by the simplicity of the geology of the area. Multiple layers of different types of material were not seen like on earth. Ninety percent of the area surveyed seemed to be a huge cavity. The naturally formed structures supporting the roof of the caves by protruding from the bottom and terminating at the top in random patterns were easily identified. The thickness of the moon's surface above the cave as measured varied from 4.5ft to 37ft. The data also indicated that the cave roof thickness was decreasing as one moved toward the signal spot and in fact the lowest thickness estimated at 3ft would be encountered exactly at the signal spot. The thickness of the layer of moon dust that covered the moon's surface varied from place to place and ranged from as little as 0.5 inch to as much as 11 ft. The base of the cavity seemed to exhibit some degree of variation but large flat areas were prominent. The surface material and the vertical supporting structures appeared to be composed of a uniform solid substance. The floor material on the caves gave readings that resembled the data of general soil found on earth, but no conclusive prediction could be made as regards its actual composition.

After referring the 3D data on the substrate of the cave, and considering several alternative locations at which to drill, the SETI-NASA team finally decided on a location 70ft away from the signal spot as their intended entry point to drill through. 70ft was thought to be an adequate distance away from the signal source spot to make a drill hole without unduly disturbing any activity that might be taking place at the signal source. The thickness of the cave roof at this location was a value of 7ft which was well within the capability of the drilling rig. The dust cover above the surface was about two inches thick at this spot. The surface material was also no different to the material at the signal spot. According to the 3D map of the cave interior, the drilling point chosen would afford a good view to a camera dropped down through the drill hole. The area around the cave as well as the area directly under the signal spot would come into very clear view. The depth to the cave bottom was 37ft from the top of the roof or the moon's surface and this distance was also well within the reach of the telescopic rod.

The drilling rig was an integral, embedded part of Master. Right now Master was 500ft away from the signal spot and to carry out the drilling Master had to be maneuvered to the exact chosen spot. Though NASA was very confident of being able to move Master to the required location using the rocket thrusters, they were concerned about the disturbance of dust which might then settle over the signal spot. However videos taken during landing indicated that the dust blown away by the thrusters settled back on the moon surface quite quickly and with only a small spread as there was no atmosphere to permit particles to drift to other areas. Therefore NASA felt there were no constraints to commencing drilling and set about the task of flying Master to the drilling spot.

Intrusion and Spying ••• ••••

Some days had passed by the time all of the preliminary tasks were completed in sequence. During this interval, the SETI-NASA team had of course continued with the normal communications routine interacting with the moon signal. They had however no way of informing the source that there was now a lunar rover and a Lander in the vicinity or to know whether the source was already aware of it. The normal signal exchange took place as usual with the codes for wake up and bye! bye! being transmitted at each session. Now however, the SETI-NASA team had feelings of excitement as well as apprehension over the possible repercussions of their well-intentioned moves which might incur the unfortunate results of being interpreted as invasive or worse, hostile.

After two days spent on brain storming, planning, simulation-testing and making the final decision, the time had come to relocate Master at the drilling spot. Master folded back Collie's ramp and got ready for takeoff. Collie remained on the ground. The reduction of weight due to Collie's 'separation' helped reduce the burden on the thruster rockets. Collie's video cameras were made ready to record the entire operation. Under command by NASA, Master moved 430ft in hovering flight and landed flawlessly at the drilling spot. As usual the SETI-NASA team expressed their emotions by their customary cheers, whoops and yells.

Collie had to climb back into Master's belly to enhance the weight effect required to counteract the up thrust while drilling. After Master leveled itself, the ramp was laid down and Collie easily found its way back in upon receiving the NASA command. Based on previous experience with lunar regolith, NASA estimated that 3 hours were needed to complete drilling. They were however not quite sure whether the material here might have a different hardness. After ensuring that the signal source of the moon was in rest mode, commands were given to Master to commence drilling. The drill was powered by Nitrogen gas driven motors supported on electrically activated operating arms. There was no plan to recover core material to take back to earth. The adopted mode for drilling was to pulverize the material as drilling took place and not to extract a solid core which might fall in to the cave at the end of drilling and lead to unforeseeable consequences. The pulverized dust was to be automatically extracted using the same Nitrogen expended in the drill.

As a preliminary task prior to drilling, Master operated its gas jets to blow away all the dust from its base. The SETI-NASA team did not want any moon dust to fall into the cave even accidentally on penetration. After boring down into the first inch the material was tested by the onboard analyzers and the results were relayed to earth. The specialists who had designed the drill found that the material was harder than lunar regolith but it was yet well within the ability of the drill to penetrate and therefore the drill was operable though at a reduced rate. The estimated drilling time was re-evaluated at 5 hours considering the increased hardness and slightly lowered drilling speed to be employed and Master was commanded to continue drilling.

After 3 hours into the process of drilling, the SETI-NASA team was informed by "Hi!", that the signal source was issuing the wakeup signal. The SETI-NASA team stopped the drilling immediately and responded with the signal to say Hello! ... Everybody's attention immediately diverted to the source signal, wondering if it was an indication of trouble. But nothing unusual was noticed. After around an hour of the usual signal exchanges, the source signaled "Bye! Bye!" and the session terminated. The SETI-NASA team was somewhat confused as regards the next step to be taken and suspended drilling operations for two days after which they decided that the only way forward was to continue with the drilling.

Drilling thus commenced again, and as predicted full penetration was achieved after slightly less than 2 more hours of drilling. The last stage of the drilling operation included provision to cause a draft-suction flow to make the particles flow away from the drill hole and ensure that none would fall into the cave. The drill rig also had provision to lower a felt curtain at the bottom of the hole to prevent any dust or light from outside entering the cave. As the drilling operation had been satisfactorily completed, Collie's weight was no longer required and it was moved out of Master to revert to its own assigned tasks.

Immediately upon completion of drilling, the sensor mounted head of an investigation probe was slowly inserted into the cave using the telescopic arm. The probe comprised a micro video camera, high resolution camera and various sensors to assess the physical and chemical nature of the interior of the cave. The probe head was stationed protruding just a few inches below the inner roof surface of the cave. This was of course a precautionary step to minimize possibility of detection. The video camera was aimed in the direction of the signal spot. As had been anticipated, what the SETI-NASA team saw through the camera was the illumination from their own red LASER beam that was strikingly bright against the dim surroundings. Other than the LASER beam they saw very many streams of light entering the cave from background areas. The light sensitivity of the camera had also to be adjusted to see the other objects around. The SETI-NASA team saw some equipment located where the LASER beam fell on the ground in the cave. They presumed that these were the radio and light signal sources. No moving objects were visible. Gas chromatograph analysis indicated the presence of water and oxygen. The sensors in the probe that sniffed the cave atmosphere indicated 78% humidity. Gases were recorded at 88.7% Oxygen, 5.4% Carbon dioxide, 3.2% Nitrogen, 1.5 % Methane and remainder of 1.2 % other gases. The microphone in the probe picked up various sounds, indicating the cave was not silent. The Camera was now turned slowly to make an initial scan of the cave's inner area. Even before the camera reached a 25 degree rotation the SETI-NASA team had a gut-feeling that it was a living habitat. Within a few minutes they realized that the cave they were looking into was not of typical cave that one came across on earth. It was in fact a key component of an entire different format. Suddenly the camera captured a bird flying across the cave from a small shrub nearby. This was the first confirmatory evidence of life on/in the moon. The SETI-NASA team was overjoyed and overwhelmed imagining how the public would react to this news. The bird now flew towards the camera, pecked at it and alighted on the camera in an act of curiosity. Luckily the camera suffered no damage! The bird peeped into the lens, blinding the camera for a few seconds and then flew away. The video camera was now zoomed to distant locations. To everyone's utter amazement a large pool of liquid water seemingly located around 150 feet from the probe came into view. The water in the pool was shimmering. It took some time for the team to realize that it was due to the reflection of the glowing roof of the cave above the lake. The pool was surrounded by vegetation. A closer look at the shrubs around the water pool showed them to be radically different from what is found on earth. Tiny waves appeared on the water surface making typical, mellow wave sounds. On one of the rock pillars near the water pool, there were some pictorial scripts resembling the hieroglyphs in the Egyptian pyramids. Close up pictures taken by zooming onto these signs showed up the details clearly but did not signify anything to the team. The surrounding areas appeared to be purpose sculptured into dwellings and areas for gatherings with steps, benches, platforms, podiums etc... None of these resembled the ancient structures found in Rome or elsewhere, but seemed to have a unique style depicting a dwellers' culture. The dwellings resembled man made houses caved out of rocks found in many parts of our world. There were long narrow meandering pathways extending beyond the range of view of the camera, resembling pathways commonly seen in hilly terrain. At several places there were big clay pots presumably for storage of water. All this visual information was obtained by viewing in the existing soft light condition in the cave. The special lights carried in the probe and in the camera were not switched on, so as not to leave room for detection.

NASA extended the probe further down to obtain greater viewing access of partially hidden areas. Probably the same bird pecked at the camera again and flew away. Suddenly the probe picked up the sound of voices from the cave. NASA immediately issued a command to make the probe head to its original position. Looking in the direction of the voices, they saw something that shook them to their very core. Beings with a basic resemblance of form to people on earth! About 200 feet away from the camera, they saw four of such persons carrying a boat like object. After a few seconds, they disappeared from view as they moved on to an area outside the field of view of the camera. This was another shattering moment of wonder and joy to the team. Their eyes were glued to the computer monitors and HDTV screens and they immediately replayed the recorded parts of what they had just seen. The cloths these people wore appeared to be all the same kind of uniform, all of the same color. The SETI-NASA team thought they were about five and a half feet tall. They walked with a slow and easy gait in somewhat like the bouncing style of Neil Armstrong's walk on the moon.

With every passing second, the SETI-NASA team found more and more exciting things as the pictures registered on their high definition screens. They realized that the funding of their project was now more than justified and all their hard work was fully rewarded. The public who watched all these streaming videos were astonished and gratified.

All these observations were made when communication with the moon signal was in rest mode. The next regular signal exchange exercise was to start in just 10 minutes. The camera was focused back to the signal spot. So far nobody had been seen around the equipment which was covered under what appeared to be a sheet of fabric resembling canvas.

The SETI-NASA team still could not rule out the possibility that the signals were remotely activated. Within a few short minutes they would know the answer. The SETI-NASA team was very eagerly watching if any moon people might arrive to man the equipment and activate signal transmission. If there were people operating the equipment, would they see the spy camera? What might be their reaction if they saw the camera? Might they attempt to destroy the probe head? How could all the media information that SETI-NASA installed on "Master" be delivered to the moon people in a friendly manner? Should they retract the probe if the moon people tried to examine it? These were the questions going round in the minds of some of the key team members.

Dooda & Loola ••• ••••

Five minutes had passed and "Hi!" was getting ready to transmit the wakeup call. Suddenly the camera captured two people walking slowly towards the signal spot. They wore the same uniform like clothes that were worn by the four people observed earlier. They carried a number of objects in their hands. The camera was able to obtain sharper pictures of their faces. The NASA-SETI team found that these people were almost perfectly white in color. They seemed identical at first glance but on closer examination it was possible to make out specific differences. They had eyes that shone with a greenish glow.

You know that these two were none other than Dooda and Loola. Let us see what happened next.

The two moon people removed the canvas like cover on the equipment. The equipment had a bulky belly-like base from which jutted out a long protruding portion of around 5 feet, in similar fashion to the way long telephoto lenses stick out from a camera. The SETI-NASA team concluded that this was their light signal generating unit. There were three stools nearby that were covered. The two moon people removed the covers and sat on the stools. They started writing something on the clipboard like devices that both of them had in their hands. The SETI-NASA team presumed that they were getting ready for the beaming in of the coded LASER signal.

"Hi!" was getting ready to activate transmission of the LASER beam. At the same time Master's video camera was got into readiness to observe the various reactions of the people in the cave. After completely shutting off the beam for about five minutes, a long "dash" signal that lasted about 10 seconds was transmitted. When the LASER beam was off the intensity of lighting in the cave dropped considerably. The SETI-NASA team saw the two people sitting by their instrument and looking at each other. They now manipulated their instrument to generate their light signal which was of an extremely bright pale blue color. This beam was about an inch in diameter as opposed to the 0.3 inch diameter LASER signal. It was crisp, bright and impressive and looked very much like a LASER beam. It was a "dash" signal! This was a huge relief for the SETI-NASA team as they now knew exactly what was happening at the moon end and brought to an end the uncertainty of the past two years. Meanwhile Collie was positioned at a distance so as to be able to observe the moon's light signal while being on the moon's surface. The SETI-NASA team continued their usual signal exchanges while observing exactly what the two moon people were doing. It was apparent that these two were following the signals very seriously. It looked as if they were taking down notes, discussing things from time to time and setting about their tasks meticulously. On occasions when the SETI-NASA team deliberately sent confusing signals, the puzzled reactions of the two people was immediately apparent. In one instance, one of them got up from his seat and walked towards the other and said something while pointing with his finger to the note pad. When the SETI-NASA team restored the normal status quo they seemed relieved and happily continued responding as before. It was clear that they were talking to each other from the time they were there. As their voice levels were picked up very faintly at the probe head, only parts of their conversations were audible to the earth station. The language they used was strange and had a sing-song style with words that seemed to the SETI-NASA team to be spoken in a long dragged-on manner. The signal exchange ended after 45 minutes with the Bye! Bye! signal. The two people covered their light emitting instrument with the canvas type cover and headed away in the same direction they had come from. The camera followed them until the view was obstructed by a wide vertical rock structure. The SETI-NASA team knew that they would be seeing these two after about 24 hours at the next session. It was a great relief and joy that the two moon people did not notice the probe head.

In keeping with the decisions taken at the planning stage the SETI-NASA team would as far as possible avoid acts that would reveal their presence to the moon people until they had obtained enough information to solve the mystery of the radio wave. They would have to wait 4 more days for the usual 14th day radio signal to be generated. It had by this time become clear to the SETI-NASA team that the moon people must have other equipment than they had so far seen, that transmitted the radio waves.

Over the next few days very many scenes of the males and females of the moon people who came within view of the video camera were captured. On one occasion, two people were observed filling the big storage pots with water. These two persons were women. Though members of both sexes wore identical dresses, the difference between men and woman could be identified easily by the unique marker that was the beard that all the men had. The people on earth who viewed the recordings of the video cameras could also clearly hear the voices of the moon people and the sounds of birds and insects when these were emitted close to the camera.

The video streams were continuously broadcast to the public by many TV channels and dedicated web sites. Contrary to the doomsday predictions of many pundits no panic was observed anywhere in the world due to the discovery of the moon. People all around the world were keen to know more about the moon people and their living environment than in expressing negative sentiments. Presumably, the people on the earth might have been calm due to their understanding that earth's people were far superior to those of the moon. The video evidence so far relayed led to the widespread public presumption that the moon's people were hundreds if not a thousand years behind us. Most people envisaged future manned missions to meet the moon dwellers in person. There was a building up of various vivid speculations of what such encounters would result in. The discovery of life on the moon provided a huge incentive to many companies interested in venturing into establishing future moon colonies. The proof of the presence of liquid water, oxygen and animals in the moon was a very powerful source of motivation.

Why life on or in the moon was not discovered earlier during the Apollo missions puzzled many people. People also wondered whether the moon people were only restricted to this isolated location at which they had been spotted. If so what about the other areas and what would be the population? Suddenly there was a host of questions to be pondered over in ever increasing numbers. What do they eat? How are their children raised? What type of social life do they have? Do they have elections?

Who leads the community? Are there kings or presidents? Are there animals? How much water do they have? What are their religions or do they have only one or none? Are they kind or arrogant? Are they intelligent? What sort of vehicles do they use? Where do they really live? What type of rituals do they perform? What is their life span? Do they practice polygamy or monogamy? Do they get sick? What type of diseases do they have? How do they produce light? What about electricity and other types of energy sources? These were a small fraction from the enormous list of questions people had.

Mystery of Radio Signal   •••   ••••

The SETI-NASA teams had very many brain storming sessions to plan future action in interacting with the moon people. They were keen to get it right at the first go and could not afford to jeopardize the years of hard work that they had devoted to their goals. Their biggest present concern was whether the moon people might destroy their probe head. If everything worked out as planned, "Master" carried with it a large array of items that would be useful to establish a relationship with the moon people. If the moon people were repulsed by any of the initial moves, all the hard work and planning could go up in smoke.

During the two days past, both parties had their light signal exchange sessions as usual. About 10 hours prior to the moon's scheduled 14 day radio transmission time, the SETI-NASA teams observed a major increase of moon people passing through the area within view of the probe's camera. A count indicated a figure in excess of 500 people. Everyone who came to the area looked at the incoming LASER beam and the equipment installed in the cave as they had never seen anything like these before. Most people had fun touching the LASAR beam though the area was cordoned off with a rope. At one time, there were about 50 people in the area; some were seated, some were eating food that they had brought with them, others were sleeping or looking around idly and a few were chatting. The mood and movement seemed to resemble a group of persons on holiday taking time to relax. Each of them had a small carrying case hanging at their backs or on their shoulders. About 6 hours prior to the moon's scheduled 14 day radio transmission time all the people left the vicinity. The people all moved in one chosen direction. A few hours later, the same two people who performed the light signal routine came to the signal spot. Shortly thereafter, they were joined by three more people who carried a device in a hand stretcher like carrier. The SETI-NASA teams were quick to realize that this would be the radio transmitter. The SETI-NASA teams could see the equipment clearly after the cover was removed. The equipment seemed to be wrapped with tape and had a detachable part that looked like an old fashioned turret gun about 2ft long. The three people who came later erected a tower that looked like a scissors lift. They attached the detachable part to the top of the scissors lift. The detachable part was also connected to the main equipment by wires. These wires were shiny and seemed bare and without insulation. The clearance between the detachable part to the cave roof was around 10 feet. All five persons were involved in the activity of setting up. The SETI-NASA team realized that they were getting ready to transmit the radio signal.

Collie was getting ready on the moon's surface to video record the dust movement at the top. The video camera on the probe showed moon people coming into the cave again in large numbers. A few electrical discharge arcs that emanated from the detachable unit indicated that the radio transmission was on. This was confirmed immediately by receipt of a signal at the earth station. The three assistants kept moving the tower by small increments in one direction. The video relayed by Collie confirmed the movement of the dust at the upper surface of the moon immediately above the signal spot. The probe too detected a high level of electromagnetic energy emanating from the moon scientists' equipment. Meanwhile in a steady and continuous stream, moon people flowed pass the area in great numbers. They all had their eyes focused on what their scientists were doing and on the incoming LASER beam. The two scientists explained what they had been doing. The happy and light spirited moon people did not seem to care very much about what the two scientists were saying and hopped on. Probably they did not have enough time to listen to them as they bounced along at speed. It would seem that "They were in a different world". Because of the incessant chatter of the people passing by, the whole cave was very noisy at that time.

The signal session lasted about 70 minutes. At the end of the session the two scientists were talking at length with each other with their hands pointing up a few times to the roof of the cave right above the signal spot. The assistants too joined the conversation. The tower on the scissors lift was brought down and the transmission equipment was moved out. The SETI-NASA team did not have to spend much time in figuring out what was happening. They realized that these two scientists had discovered a method of displacing the dust on the moon's surface. They would be performing this task on every fourteenth successive day. Why not on other days was a question. The SETI-NASA team realized that this exercise must be of very great importance and significance to the moon people as removal of dust would help bring more sunlight into the cave. It was thus seen as likely that there were no coded messages in the radio waves. Glitches or cyclic procedures during the transmission such as switching and changing of batteries or perhaps purposely switching on and off the signal to boost the dust move, could be causing effects mimicking coded messages. The SETI-NASA team also realized that the two scientists should be very intelligent for having the ability to prepare a brilliant light beam to respond to their LASER signal. The source of the powerful pale blue light beam was still a question. As to why the miniature thermal emission spectrometer on the probe did not detect any heat images from the light source, also puzzled the earth scientists. Why did people gather on that particular day in very large numbers? If they gathered to see the radio wave demonstration, why didn't they show much interest was another conundrum?

By observing the body language of the two scientists and the behavior of the other moon people, the SETI-NASA team was optimistic that they would be able to establish rapport with the moon people. They decided on trying out moves to get the attention of the two scientists on the next day.

As usual, on the next day, the two scientists sat at their places anticipating the wakeup call. The signal exchange took place and went on for about five minutes. After that the SETI-NASA team sent the "Hello!" signal (long "dash") three times to mean "Hello! Hello!, Hello!" though it was not in the usual signal protocol. Through the probe camera the SETI-NASA team observed that the moon scientists were puzzled as to why they got this unusual signal at the middle of their regular signal exercise. They saw the two scientists talking to each other. The two scientists too repeated the "hello!" signal. The SETI-NASA team stopped their LASER beam transmission. After about two minutes, the moon scientists started sending light signals as they were in desperation to restore the LASER signal. They also then stopped their action and were talking to each other and looking up for the signal. At this moment the probe fired a LASER beam with a "Hello" signal. Immediately both scientists turned their eyes in the direction of the probe. The SETI-NASA team was able to take good pictures of their faces this time. The Moon scientists were surprised to see another LASER beam coming at them from inside the cave. The probe kept on beaming the usual signal pattern that was used on the earlier days. The two scientists seemed to be stunned. They did not reply, move or talk to each other for about five minutes. A few times they took their eyes off the probe to look in the direction from which the LASER beam used to come. They rubbed their eyes with their knuckles a few times. One of the scientists commenced to walk towards the probe and signaled the other to follow him.

The two scientists were looking wide eyed at the probe which was about 25ft above the ground surface they were now standing on. They began to talk to each other and their conversation was picked up clearly and listened to intently by the SETI-NASA team. After about 15 minutes the SETI-NASA team stopped the LASER beam transmission from the probe. The SETI-NASA team now saw one of the scientists saying something to the other. It seemed to be an instruction as the scientist who listened went back to the light signal source and sent out a "Hello!" signal. This was done with their light probe still directed at the cave roof on the moon's surface. The SETI-NASA team replied with a "Hello!" signal from the probe. The signaling session continued as usual while one scientist was watching from directly under the probe. After 20 minutes the SETI-NASA team deliberately stopped transmitting the LASER beam. The two scientists were together now. They were wondering why the signal stopped. They sent a few "Hello!" signals but the SETI-NASA team did not respond. They tried again and again desperately. They were looking up and in the direction of the probe, but observed that there was no response. The SETI-NASA team then saw the two scientists trying to rotate the light signal in the direction of the probe. They finally repositioned it and sent a "Hello!" signal towards the probe. The SETI-NASA team responded immediately through the probe's LASER beam. The moon scientists and the SETI-NASA team were both overjoyed. They continued their signal session. The usual LASER signal they received from over the signal spot did not appear any more. The signaling continued solely via the probe.

The SETI-NASA team was very happy as they were able to transfer the attention of the moon scientists to the probe and also establish their probe as the new communications center. This was part of the master plan of the SETI-NASA team as will be explained later. At the end of the signaling session just after the Bye! Bye! signal, the SETI-NASA team decided to drop into the cave a poster stored in Master along with a number of other information exchange accessories. Before dropping the poster in, the probe's LASER beam fired several blinker signals to get the scientists attention. Using the retractable telescopic rod, the poster was lowered and dropped into the cave gently. One of the scientists quickly moved forward and collected the poster while the other was looking eagerly at the telescopic rod retracting back to the top of the cave. It seemed like magic to him. Before they opened the rolled up poster, both scientists gazed at the probe in amazement and their body language seemed to signify "Hey! What is going on here?" The video camera showed the two scientists taking a quick peek at the poster which however they did not open fully and examine. Instead they went back to gaping at the probe. After about 10 minutes they went away with the poster.

The poster was an extension of the idea of the gold plated plaque carried by the Pioneer 10 space craft, which had by now ventured beyond the edge of our solar system. The poster was printed double sided and in color and made of indestructible fire resistant material of texture similar to paper. It had the picture of a naked man and woman copied from the original gold plated plaque. The man's hand was raised in a gesture of greeting and good will. It had the color pictures of the solar system with a small moon revolving round the earth. There was a big picture of the earth and the moon in color with an arrow indicating that the man and the woman are from the earth. Also in one picture, a curved arrow indicated the robot mission from earth to the moon. There were pictures showing the moon from earth and also pictures taken of the earth by the Apollo astronauts when they were on the moon. The middle portion was devoted to the present mission. There was a cross sectional view of the cave also showing the LASER beam coming from the satellite. Further, the light beam coming out of the moon's signal spot was also indicated. Just below the cross sectional picture, "dot" and "dash" signals were depicted using florescent paint to give a luminous look. A little lower down, all the signals that were exchanged daily was outlined. This row started with the "Hello!" signal and ended with the "Bye! Bye!" signal. Next came the pictures of "Master" and "Collie" on the moon's surface. Finally there was another large cross sectional picture depicting the drill hole, the probe, Master and Collie and the new LASER beam issuing from the probe. At the very bottom

103

there were many stamp sized pictures of men and women from many cultures, animals, birds, fish, insects, trees, water ways, landscapes and dwellings and commercial buildings. At the planning stages of the project this was one of the ideas put forward and unanimously agreed upon. The SETI-NASA team believed that these pictures would help any living beings who had the ability to transmit a radio signal, to acquire a broad understanding of what was going on.

Dooda and Loola Informing the Elders ••• ••••

Dooda and Loola made a beeline to their research station, with Dooda carrying the poster. They were shocked at what they had experienced in the past few hours. They knew they had a very heavy responsibility to inform the elders in Daaadi City about this immediately. Their curiosity to study the poster was however much more urgent to them than of informing the elders of the incidents of the day. Their patience ran out, both Dooda and Loola decided to quickly examine the poster. It took some time but little by little they could understand the message in it. They did not waste time on investigating their familiar "dot" and "dash" signal patterns outlined in the pictures. They now knew that there was some kind of equipment stationed above the place at which they saw the second red light signal. They also guessed that the same equipment had drilled through the surface to insert the rod that held the second red light source. They further knew that the poster was dropped through the drilled hole by the same equipment on top. After seeing the picture of Collie, Dooda and Loola concluded that there must be another piece of equipment on the moon's surface above. They recognized the sun but could not understand the picture of the solar system to make sense of it and thought they should ask one of their astronomers. The picture of the earth was a familiar one to many people on the moon including Dooda and Loola. This was the place they believed to be their heaven. Dooda and Loola understood immediately that the signals and the pieces of equipment at the top all had something to do with the heaven. The events and the poster were greatly exciting to both of them. They were highly thrilled and could not believe what had taken place. The news spread to all the people working in the research facility in double quick time. Dooda and Loola ran back to see the probe once more before going to inform the elders of all they saw and experienced that day. More colleagues of Dooda and Loola joined them at the place directly below where the probe was located. They could not see very much of the probe. Their colleagues spent more time there after Dooda and Loola hurried to summon the elders. The SETI-NASA team observed all these events but kept the probe motionless and inactive.

Within about two hours, Dooda managed to summon five highly respected elders who had helped him in the past to carry on with the light signal transmission. Dooda and Loola explained everything that had happened. The explanation was made whilst standing under the probe. Apart from the elders, there were more scientists from the research facility. The people carried in additional bright lights to illuminate the area better. Dooda showed them the probe which was inactive at that time. Dooda and Loola showed the elders the poster including the picture of heaven. Both of them told the elders that the pieces of equipment in the pictures had some connection to heaven according to the depiction. The quality of the poster and the clarity of the pictures were more than adequate to convince the elders that the poster had a connection to heaven, as they had never seen a quality print or material of the type the poster was made of ever at all in their lives before. All of them touched the poster and looked at the pictures on both sides very many times. It was not very clear what they all finally made of it or if they understood any of It! The elders were invited to be present for the next signal exchange session.

As unknown to the moon people, the camera was still on; the SETI-NASA team saw everything that took place. As the elders were seen to be assisted by others to negotiate the steps and walk around, the SETI-

NASA team understood that the five persons addressed by Dooda and Loola were elderly persons. They however wore the same uniform-like clothes. The SETI-NASA team was not sure what type of bright light the moon people used to boost the luminosity in the cave. It appeared that one type was of very shiny and crystalline appearance and was about the size and shape of a large avocado pear. The thermal imaging camera captured the body heat images of all the people who were there but did not detect any heat emanated by the light source. This fact puzzled the scientists of SETI-NASA. "It is very strange!" thought the experts.

Dooda and Loola could not sleep that day due to the excitement caused by the images whirling in their heads. Dooda was impatiently awaiting the next signal exchange occasion and hoped it would come sooner. Every passing minute felt ten times exaggerated to him. This impatience was equally felt by many of the scientists in the SETI-NASA team, though the two groups were separated by hundreds of thousands of miles. Dooda was so impatient, once he asked Loola if he would like to go with him to send a wake up signal ahead of the scheduled signal time. Loola pointed out that they needed to wait for the elders.

Loola, the five elders, several colleagues from the research facility and Dooda assembled at the signal spot several minutes before the scheduled signal time. A few sat close to Dooda and Loola at the signaling spot, some were seated on the floor close to the probe head and some others were scattered around. Altogether there were twenty three persons. The gathering looked like one in a men's club as there were no women to be seen. A few minutes before the scheduled time, Dooda directed towards the probe, a wakeup call using Loola's light apparatus. The probe replied with a LASER signal immediately. Thereafter they got on with their normal signal exchange process. Though most of the elders had seen the former LASER signal, they were excited. They were expecting more posters to drop, from the probe but met with disappointment as no new posters appeared.

After about 5 minutes, the SETI-NASA team decided to get on with the new moves they had planned. The SETI-NASA team sent commands to Master to lower the probe by five feet. It was still out of reach of the moon people to be open to damage. The usual signal exchange was continued from this new position. The moon people who were there saw the probe coming down. They were mesmerized and excited to see this extraordinary gadgetry. Dooda wondered momentarily whether he should re-target his light signal at the probe, as it was below the original level. But he realized immediately, that action was not necessary as the red signal was still responding without a break. Dooda however could not understand how the probe achieved this. After 5 minutes the probe was completely retracted by Master. The moon people expected a poster drop and wondered what was next? All eyes were sharply focused at the spot where the probe had been. The telescopic rod came back with another attachment. Bit by bit this attachment which was in folded form began to open out. When it opened out completely, it formed into a 12in x 21in television screen. A picture took shape and appeared on the screen. This picture was identical to the first page of the poster delivered to the moon people the previous day. The screen looked outstandingly bright and clear against the dim background in the cave. All who were present were eager to come closer to have a better look but they were also somewhat hesitant and undecided. It took nearly 20 minutes for the people who were initially stunned to get over their apprehension and finally settle down to congregate in front of the TV screen. The SETI-NASA team did not change the static picture for up to 25 minutes. During this period, the SETI-NASA team observed an initial silence and then gradual chatter that turned in a very short time into a loud cacophony of the moon people,. The picture on the screen was then replaced by the picture on the reverse side of the poster. The moon people were surprised at how it changed so quickly. Thereafter at one minute intervals the picture was flipped from front side to reverse alternatively. Dooda, Loola and some of the elders had facial expressions that were very difficult to interpret, as they either carried elements of excitement or caution or both. The moon people really enjoyed what they saw as none of them had ever seen anything like this before. Ten minutes later, the SETI-NASA team made the live video stream that they were capturing from the cave, to appear on the screen in a "picture in a picture" format. The moon people immediately realized that it was they who were now on the screen. They started expressing their joy in various ways including using loud words. After a little while the SETI-NASA team turned on the speakers on the probe and the moon people realized that they could hear their own voices too from the probe when they talked loud. They found it a greatly amusing and unique experience to be able to play with the sound and videos.

When the SETI-NASA team zoomed the lens on Dooda, his face appeared large and clear on the screen. All those gathered immediately looked at him. The SETI-NASA team repeated this procedure with each and every person who was there for strategic purposes and everyone had the opportunity to enjoy seeing their picture appearing on the screen. As these events were taking place, more and more people gathered to see the strange events taking place in the cave.

The SETI-NASA team next placed a picture of the moon in the background with the moon people in the foreground, to indicate that they were from the moon; but the team was not sure whether the moon people would understood the message that they were trying to convey. As the moon people had never seen the moon from outer space it was not to be expected that they would identify the picture of the moon as being of their world. Then one after another, a few pictures of the earth taken from various satellites were projected. As mentioned before, the moon people identified the earth as heaven. Most of the moon people who were at this gathering had physically seen this "Earth Heaven". The SETI-NASA team kept on projecting faces of men and woman from various cultures on the earth to emphasize that these were the mix of people living on earth. The moon people wondered why these people were of different color and also very different from them in complexion. Finally the SETI-NASA team played a video of an infant and the stages of a human's growth; the growth process from infant to child, child to adult and then ageing. The pictures included men and women in static and dynamic media formats. The moon people keenly watched this presentation and thought that all these people must be from a different world. They presumed that they could certainly not be inhabitants of the heaven that they believed in. If they were from heaven the moon people expected them to be all young, happy looking, beautiful and of single color.

The SETI-NASA team then screened the video stream taken by Collie. It showed how Master was stationed on top of the moon's surface. Collie's camera console was made to rotate 360 degrees at slow speed to give a good panoramic view of the moon's surface and the dark gaps of space. Dooda and Loola being naturally very intelligent readily understood what it was they were watching. They had to explain to the others what they were seeing as none of them had seen the moon surface in that fashion. Collie's camera was focused on the signal spot. The SETI-NASA team activated a LASER beam from "Hi!" which immediately penetrated into the cave through the original signal spot. Collie's video capture showed how the red signal penetrated the transparent moon surface. Upon seeing the LASER beam inside the cave at that moment, Dooda and Loola quickly grasped the cause of the whole chain of events that took place around them during the past several months. But they still could not grasp as to where the original red beam was coming from, though they saw the picture of the satellite in the poster. However now they understood what was what; basically the probe, Master, Collie and the other interactive things that they had seen so far. Dooda and Loola saw the surface of the signal spot area when Collie focused the camera on it. They identified the clear glass like surface area and the dust filled areas. When Collie started roving around, the moon people were amazed again, as anything motorized was a great novelty to them. They wondered how Collie could move around the moon surface without anybody in it. Let us hope they will get to know all these eventually!

109

The moon people were glued to the screen and were already in a dream world. They saw an animated video next, demonstrating how the Delta III rocket brought "Hi!" to the moon orbit and how it was firing the LASER beam at the signal spot. Dooda and Loola had no difficulty at all to follow and understand the whole story very well. They understood that the original red beam that they received was emitted by an object parked far away in space. At this stage Dooda and Loola were interested in trying to understand how Master and Collie came to the moon. Intuitively, the next animated video planned by the SETI-NASA team, illustrated exactly what Dooda and Loola wanted to know. It demonstrated how Master and Collie were ensconced in the Delta 3 rocket, the rocket launch, exiting from earth orbit, descending of Master onto the moon surface, soft landing, Collie leaving Master's belly and roving around, Master performing the drilling work, telescopic rod movement, activating the 2nd LASER beam and finally unfolding of the TV screen.

As will be easy to now understand, technically the SETI-NASA team could even transmit CNN news over the screen. However the primary and all important aim was for the SETI-NASA team to get the two scientists to interact with them over the audio and video interfaces in the system. The advantage of the audio video system was that they could send any audiovisual material to suit the particular situation. All these were a preplanned set of strategies designed to handle a number of potential scenarios that they envisaged.

Seth & Max ••• ••••

Dooda and Loola pretty much understood that they were dealing with people from another world. They also understood that these people were technologically very advanced. The video they saw on the rocket and the spacecraft were the evidence. At this stage Dooda and Loola did not have a steady mind set as to what to do or not do and simply kept on observing the screen.

As a next stage in the interaction, the SETI-NASA team projected the still pictures of Seth Sagan and Max Glenn, side by side on the screen. From the inception, Seth Sagan headed the SETI branch of the project and Max Glenn headed the NASA branch of the project as joint executive officers. All SETI-NASA team project staff came under the combined umbrella of command of Seth and Max. Below their pictures on the screen the "Hello!" sign was shown in red and it was blinking with long pauses to indicate "Hello!" For Dooda and Loola the sign was still a wakeup call not a conventional "Hello!". Then Seth and Max appeared live. First Seth and then Max said Hello! to the moon crowd. The audio effects were on. This was done several times with traditional Japanese style repeated bows. Seth and Max had observed in the past video recordings that the moon people after bowing to each other as an act of courtesy also touched each other's shoulders at the same time with their right hands. Seth and Max shock hands with each other and then touched the shoulders of each other. After that both of them bent over and extended their right hands towards the camera to indicate that they would like to do the same with the moon people.

The video stream relayed to earth by the probe, showed that all the moon people in the cave were gathered round the five elders who were together at one spot. First, the elders were seen discussing amongst themselves and then they appeared to be directing questions at Dooda and Loola. Their body language indicated this clearly. On the screen, the pictures of Seth and Max were placed still and silent as the team knew that the elders were yet discussing something important with Dooda and Loola. The "Picture in picture" also showed the live picture of the discussion that was taking place. The picture from the cave was made larger than the picture of Seth and Max. At one time Dooda and Loola took prominent roles in the discussion as they seemed to be explaining matters to the elders. Their hands and body gestures indicated they were stressing some important issues. Their conversation was clearly heard by the SETI-NASA team. The voices were useful for the sub-team on earth who were working hard to learn the moon language.

At the end of the long discussion all five elders walked up to the camera, bent over a bit and raised their right hands towards the probe. Seth and Max reciprocated immediately by bowing and raising their hands to shoulder touching height, to indicate they were with them, though they were physically very far apart. This was the "Peace Pipe" moment that they were waiting for, thought the entire SETI-NASA team. Dooda and Loola repeated the elders' act. Seth and Max reciprocated immediately with wide smiles on their faces. Then the entire group of moon people gathered there raised their hands. Seth and Max reciprocated again. Seth and Max next saw the moon people greeting each other by touching each other's shoulders with their right hands. Seth and Max did the shoulder touching greeting between the two of them. Everyone's eyes were still on the screen. When the moon people saw Seth and Max greeting each other, emulating their culture, the silence in the cave broke to the sound of laughter, joy and cheering. Seth and Max shook hands and kept holding hands. The moon people started shaking hands between themselves, doubling the laughter and the fun that they felt. The SETI-NASA team realized that earth bound humans had thus introduced a change in the social customs of the moon people. Perhaps this could be regarded as Seth's small step following on Neil Armstrong's "Small step….Giant leap" legacy.

Seth appeared again. He pointed at himself with his forefinger and said "Seth". Max did the same and said "Max". After Seth repeated this action three times Dooda explained to the others that those words could be the names of the earth people. From Dooda's reaction the SETI-NASA team understood that Dooda probably understood the message. As such they projected the zoomed picture of Dooda on the screen. Dooda pointed his forefinger to himself and said "Dooda". Seth and Max clapped to convey their appreciation. The people in the cave too clapped and made joyful sounds. Loola's picture was zoomed and screened next. He said "Loola". This procedure was kept going on. There were some camera shy people too. "The tone of every one's voice was the same", thought the SETI-NASA team.

At the end of the introductory session, pictures of Seth and Dooda were put on the screen. Seth said "Dooda" by pointing his finger towards Dooda's picture. Seth had a background crew holding placards etc., showing the names of moon people, to help him. So he did not have to memorize all the names. Dooda did not catch his name, when Seth said it first. The linguistic experts in the team corrected Seth and advised him to try again with a dragging accent. This time when Seth said "Dooooda", Dooda responded with a bow. Seth bowed too. Seth said "Seth" by pointing his finger to himself. After Seth repeated his name a few times, Dooda correctly said "Seth". Seth smiled, bowed down and clapped. This was repeated with Loola, the 2nd scientist in the moon. He pronounced Seth's name in one go. This whole exercise was repeated with everybody who introduced themselves by bowing at them. Max took over from Seth and repeated the exercise to introduce him. From time to time the background crew would come close to Max to exchange a few words. At the end of the session Seth and Max introduced "Yesha" the female member of the team. The Moon people realized she was female. Dooda, Loola and a few others pronounced her name properly. Dooda did not have any females within the crowd to introduce.

In the earlier instances the signal session did not go on for as long. This was a special day. About 13 hours had already elapsed from the time the elders came to the scene. Though nobody was tired or short of enthusiasm, the SETI-NASA team thought that it would be better to stop the session for the day. Just before ending the session Seth brought to the screen view about 20 of his male and female colleagues to indicate that there were more than Max and Yesha involved with him. The Bye! Bye! signal followed. This time it was not by the LASER beam but by the flashing signal on the screen and words by Seth and the whole team.

Dooda and Loola rushed back to their light beam and responded with a Bye! Bye! signal. Others waved at the probe. The SETI-NASA team observed that the elders were congregating again with Dooda and Loola. Other moon people were talking among themselves. They kept on looking at the screen though nothing appeared on it. All were there for over an hour after the Bye! Bye! Signal, then they started walking back in the direction they came from. It was not clear what sort of instructions the elders conveyed to Dooda and Loola, though the SETI-NASA team recorded all the conversations between them.

The SETI-NASA team realized that they had built up a good social foundation to build on in the future. They were eager to take it to the next level of being able to have a fuller dialogue to explore further into their life styles, living environment and many other areas almost without end. The linguistic experts who were in the SETI-NASA team compiled a list of words and probable meanings by repeated reviewing of the video clips. They had over 200 words in the list, picked from over 13 hours of video recordings. "balaaan" to look, " vadeeen" to greet/bow, "vadee" to sit, "hitteer" to stand, "enderr" to come in, "yanderr" to go, "seeyaa" for elder, "kathaaa" to speak, "nangeee" for woman, "buncheee" for friend, these were some of the words they picked up. The SETI-NASA team wanted to expand the list with the least possible delay. Seth and Max went through a few tutorial sessions to memorize these words and improve their pronunciation. The SETI-NASA team realized that understanding the moon people's language would be far easier than trying to make the moon people understand English. The SETI-NASA team had all the facilities to capture the words and compile a vocabulary as they had the help of complex computer backed instruments to fully evaluate any aspect pertaining to speech. In fact NASA even analyzed whether Seth and Max could correctly pronounce the words in moon language through advanced electronic evaluation devices. If there were no words in moon people's language for items like the "TV Screen" the team would try to introduce English words.

Dooda and Loola were given full sanction by the elders to carry on with what they were doing. The elders also informed Dooda and Loola that they would apprise the other elders in the community of the interactions with the aliens. The same five elders wanted to join them for the next day's session also as they were highly motivated by the series of events of the past session. After listening to their colleagues about the extraordinary events, more people from Dooda's research facility wanted to join him on the next day. Dooda and Loola wanted to know more about their new friends Seth, Max and other people living in this different world. Being intelligent scientists, Dooda and Loola understood how relatively ignorant they were, for not being on par with this new technology they encountered that could produce rockets and engage in inter planetary missions. They could not come to terms with the very wide gap between their knowledge and the superior knowledge of Seth and Max as it seemed to be too vast to imagine. They hoped to be able to learn a lot from Seth and Max and hence were looking forward to very eagerly to collaborating with them.

The next day, after the communications session was started everybody was in very good spirits. When Seth and Max appeared on the first screen, with Dooda and Loola on "picture in picture", Seth and Max bowed to the moon crowd and raised their right hands to indicate the extending of greetings. The moon crowd did the same, acknowledging their solidarity. Seth said "hello!" But there was no reply. After he said "Hello!" a few times Dooda and the others said "Hello!". The language experts surmised that there was no equivalent word for "Hello" in the moon language. Seth and Max got into an act of emulating a moon language learning session. Seth said to Max, "vadee" (meaning sit), Max sat on the chair. Then Seth said "enderr" to Max … and Max walked towards Seth. Immediately the moon people understood that Seth and Max were speaking and acting in their language. The "picture in picture" showed that the moon people were laughing in surprise and amazement. They kept on with the simulated lesson till they exhausted all the nearly 200 words they thought they knew of moon language.

Whenever Seth and Max made a mistake all the moon people attempted to correct them thereby creating confusion. Dooda intervened and requested them all to be silent and undertook the role of correcting any language errors by Seth. In fact, later on Dooda and Loola took over the acting session to teach Seth and Max. Seth and Dooda exchanged words and carried on a very basic conversation which was seen as a great entertainment by the rest of the moon crowd.

Seth wished to ascertain whether elders are addressed in a different manner of respect such as "Mr" or "Sir" and made an enquiry on how they should be addressed after introducing the picture of an elder on the screen. But the feedback indicated that there was no practice of such nature. They were all referred to by their names only irrespective of age or gender. Dooda and Loola did not have any clue about the linguistic team working behind the scenes for Seth and Max with recordings, speech analysis and other technical back up and were amazed at how Seth and Max learnt their language so quickly. In fact the 'language lab' that supported communications made it very easy for the SETI-NASA team to learn the moon people's language quickly. The SETI-NASA team now showed clips from the documentary film "The Planet Earth". The idea was to show the moon people the flora and fauna on earth for them to get a better idea of living creatures and plants on the earth and also with the idea of indicating that they would also like to see the living things in the moon. Other than for the bird that pecked on the camera on the first day, the SETI-NASA team did not see any other creature at all. The moon people enjoyed this program that lasted 30 minutes. Their deep concentration on it was evinced by rapt silence and utter immobility during the entire program. They reacted occasionally by saying things to their neighbors when some animals and their behavior was shown. Parrots, fish, primates and bats were a few of these. Some clips were played at high speed or slow motion and it is possible that the moon people might have thought that the speeds they witnessed were real speeds.

Language training sessions and various video sessions were carried out daily. Within a few weeks Seth and Max were able to have a reasonably clear conversation with Dooda and Loola. Most of the time spent in conversation was devoted to furthering of knowledge on the moon people's language, as it was very important to both parties. Over time, Dooda and Loola began to understand the functions of various units mounted on the probe head. They could identify the camera, the LASER head, microphone and other instruments. On some days both parties continued their dialogue even while having short meals. Both parties made each other understand the type of food each ate and drank via pictures projected on the TV screen. Dooda and Loola once showed samples of the water plants from which they made food. On many occasions passing onlookers had brought with them pet birds, domestic animals and a few personal goods that the SETI-NASA had looked on at with great fascination. After the SETI-NASA team felt fully confident that their probe and screen would not be damaged by the moon people they lowered the probe head to a distance within 9 feet from the ground. As a precautionary measure however it was equipped with a built-in sensor which could activate immediate retraction if anything were to approach within 3ft of it. Graphically this was illustrated to Dooda and Loola and they understood. Dooda helped Seth to confirm that the sensor circuit was working properly by deliberate triggering of the sensor. When Dooda and Loola were not around, the screen retracted and set itself at a higher elevation. Seth and Max were keen to have a closer look at the illuminating device that was used in their light signals. To convey this message they used the screen to draw a sketch of the compound optical signal unit and explained to Dooda by word as well as action that it was a unit that they were very eager to see. Loola showed them the big Babaloniums crystal that provided light to their equipment. When the full cover was completely removed from the Babaloniums crystal, the entire cave was lit up. To prevent prolonged diffusion of light in all directions, Loola covered the crystal again reverting it to its former state. Once again it was not captured by the thermal imaging unit as a heat producing object. The SETI-NASA team realized that this unit and the avocado sized object they brought with them to illuminate the cave on the first day must be of the same material. Dooda explained to Seth the principle involved in triggering of a Babaloniums crystal. Seth could not understand most of the explanation. The team decided to keep the subject suspended for another day though they were very curious about it and could not make out at all what this material was.

Though both parties were reasonably comfortable in their conversations aimed at grasping fuller details of the two worlds it was still difficult to understand certain things that were being discussed. On many occasions Seth and Max used video clips to help in their explanations. For example when Seth was explaining details of buildings, cars, trees, flowers, lightning, people etc., he used video clips to great advantage. Dooda and Loola did not have similar facilities. The moon people had a device to take pictures but it was not sufficiently developed to be used in aiding their communications.

Dooda and Loola learnt more earth related information than Seth and Max and the SETI-NASA team learnt about the moon people. Through their dialogue the SETI-NASA team learnt from Dooda the background to the radio signal instrument he developed, how it was powered and the purpose of its operation. However, when Seth asked why there were so many people in that area on the radio signal transmission day, the explanation Dooda gave was very difficult to comprehend. Loola too tried to help in the explanations when he found that Seth could not understand Dooda, but their joint effort did not improve matters at all. The SETI-NASA team was briefed about the lakes, the tides, water plants, animals, fish and other things. Dooda and Loola touched on the research that they were engaged in at their facility; about the bioluminescent organisms that they developed, the types of material they produced from the water plants, about the oil they extracted from the alga, etc. Dooda once again explained to Seth how to trigger a Babaloniums crystal. How rare these were, but how widely they were used in the caves. They said if not for the Babaloniums life in the caves would be quite uncomfortable and also hazardous.

As the days passed Dooda lost interest in the dust removal exercise. Seth agreed to try to help Dooda to remove the dust by deploying Collie. The SETI-NASA team would have to work out a way to adapt Collie's capabilities to execute this task as it was not in its planned scope of tasks. Max promised to provide Dooda technical assistance to improve his equipment. Max also agreed to help Loola enhance his knowledge on telescopes and compound lenses.

People came in large numbers to see the videos on the screen when they had the 14th day functions. This was a much better wonder and fun event for them than Dooda's moon dust removal demonstration. After Seth found out that the 14th day event was some sort of a festival day, the SETI-NASA team made a special TV broadcast on these days, with a bias towards entertainment. They nevertheless retained displays of natural things like animals, rivers, forests etc. At times the elders had to command the people to move on as they sometimes tended to spend their time glued to the video displays. As time passed, Seth was concerned about the disturbance that they were creating to the moon people's festival day. The team wondered if they should terminate the broadcast on the specific 14th days. This matter was taken up with Dooda and Loola. Being people of very unassuming nature they did not indicate any objection at all to having it. The social scientists who provided advice to the SETI-NASA team however cautioned them on what was to be shown on the screens as they identified the moon people as extremely friendly and fun loving but also as being very susceptibility in terms of their inherent extreme sensitivity. The fact that the moon people were non meat eaters and did not have ill words at all in their vocabulary seemed to indicate this possibility.

The SETI-NASA team now decided that the time had come to commence implementing the next part of their plan. The next day when Seth appeared on the screen, he had a micro video camera in his hand. Seth told Dooda he had a similar camcorder in Master and that he would deliver it to him. Seth explained to Dooda how to operate it, by picking up a camera from his desk and demonstrating the basic steps. It had only three buttons to operate. Press once to record video and sound. Pressing it again will stop the recording. The next button was to play back. The third was to go back. It had a wireless connection to the probe to transmit and receive recordings. The wireless connection would work only if the camera was in close proximity, but in any event the camera was programmed to record everything that it scanned into its own memory. Seth explained to Dooda that it had about 10 hours of battery power. The time measure in hours and minutes was well understood by Dooda and Loola, as they had acquired familiarity with the digital clock that was displayed at the bottom corner of the right side of the screen. When the camera ran out of power it was to be put on the special pad on the telescopic arm. When the battery was being recharged, the probe was designed to upload all the recordings in the memory chip to earth and to clear the memory for the next round of recordings. Seth demonstrated the operation of the camcorder. He did this by taking it to many places in his office and research complex and showing what was on his camcorder screen. Dooda was made to understand, that the pictures were coming through the small camera to their screen in the cave, when he was walking around. This was re-illustrated by various video shots taken by the SETI-NASA team to ensure Dooda understood that this was a portable camcorder. Seth told Dooda, that he was interested in seeing the other parts of the moon, close up views of trees, animals, birds, lakes, how they make food, their roads, 14th day festival, research facility of Dooda and Loola, etc. Dooda and Loola could well understand why Seth was so interested in seeing these things and they agreed without reservation to accommodate all of Seth's requests.

By now, Dooda and Loola had been exposed to a considerable coverage of how people on Seth's world lived, including how people watched TV from inside their homes. They also knew about the media coverage that people on Seth's world had on the discovery of the moon people. Though the SETI-NASA team was trying to be as open as possible with Dooda and Loola, they were still cautious and selective as regards what they allowed to be shown to the moon people. This was a precautionary measure to ensure that the feelings of the moon people would never be hurt or offended by something they might see in an Earth scene.

The camera was sent down to Dooda through the inner rod of the telescopic arm. Dooda gently took it off from the seating socket in the same way he saw Seth taking it out in the video he watched before. This was the second alien item that Dooda handled after the poster. Dooda was thrilled to open the mini flap screen of the camera and press the recording button as demonstrated by Seth. To his surprise the picture was upside down. Dooda looked at the big screen. Seth corrected Dooda by making him realize that he was holding the camera upside down. Both laughed and exchanged knowing looks to share their feelings of innocent banter that words could not express. The people who were there rushed behind Dooda to see what was on the tiny camera screen. Everybody realized that the picture on the tiny screen appeared on the big screen as well. Dooda turned the camera around on the people and enjoyed the merriment it caused, just like a small child playing with a toy. He played with it for some time, possibly about 20 minutes. Loola now took the camera from Dooda's hands and played with it too. At one point he directed it towards the TV screen and to the drilled hole from where the rod was protruding down. For the first time, the SETI-NASA team had a good view of how the TV screen and the telescopic rod were set up in the cave. They now saw with joy the result of the complex and high precision task that they had executed.

From the video clips collected during the past weeks, the SETI-NASA team gathered an enormous amount of information about the moon people, their cave system, the moon's structure, Babaloniums, the lakes, tides, water plants, shrubs, animals, insects, birds, fish, dwellings, children, schools, etc. After seeing the state of parts of Dooda's research facility and assessing the innovations that Dooda and Loola had made, the SETI-NASA team realized how brilliant Dooda and Loola were as scientists. It was impressive to see their advanced written language, their knowledge of math and their exceptional capability for learning and understanding things logically.

Friendship ••• ••••

Over time Dooda, Loola, Seth, Max, the rest of the SETI-NASA team and the colleagues of Dooda's research facility developed very close bonds. Many times, Seth and Max downloaded video clips to the camcorder so that Dooda and his colleagues could watch them when they took the camcorder back to their research center. Most clips had sound dubbed in moon language as Seth's team already had a few experts who could talk very fluently in the moon language. The camcorder as well as the TV screen was used as tools to educate Dooda and his colleagues on the subjects they were interested in. Loola was interested in developing a LASER beam. Some of these lessons had to be started at fundamental levels as some science concepts were not known to the moon people. The lack of knowledge of physical materials on the earth by moon people was also recognized as a constraint. This was the case especially in respect of metals. Within the last few months the notes that Dooda and his colleagues had taken from the video teaching lessons had been enormous. Surprisingly all the moon scientists were very smart at understanding most of the theoretical and practical aspects of the teaching material that the SETI-NASA team delivered. Their thirst for knowledge could not be quenched by what was fed from the earth. Dooda, Loola and all their research colleagues greatly appreciated the knowledge they received from the earth people. They imagined that one day they would be able to develop all these novel material and gadgetry in the moon.

122

Since the SETI-NASA team was now in a better position to direct the new friends on the moon, they focused on specific study areas. They wanted to understand more and more of the moon's interior and the life of the people. To fulfill one of the requests of Seth, Dooda promised to video record an entire session of their 14th day celebrations. When this daylong event was finally recorded and downloaded to the SETI-NASA center, the team watched it right through without a break. The SETI-NASA team thought the day long festivities represented a characteristic feature of the moon people's culture, their heritage and the recollections of the moon's incredible tale of an ages-old habitation. An extraordinary feature of the festival was that all the people were the performers as well as the spectators, totally immersed in both roles at the same time. During the performance it appeared as if they were under the influence of some kind of supernatural power. The behavior of the people and the harmony they displayed in various dance performances, patterns and routines, proved that they were in essence human. All the dancing events were spectacularly beautiful. It was astounding to note that all the dance moves had been orchestrated without a designated choreographer or a leader of any sort. Dreams of hope to have an everlasting happy life were cast in the music that they played. Many times over, Seth wondered by himself whether the people of the ancient Mayan culture performed similar ritualistic dances ages ago. He wondered what sort of exotic smells the burning torches would be producing when the dancers threw handfuls of powdery material at the fires. As an unnerving thought, the SETI-NASA team debated amongst themselves whether the secret of the moon people's unity lay in the cocktail that they consumed at the commencement of the event. Seth joked with his group of wanting to get the recipe of the cocktail, if possible from Dooda to try it out privately. Also to develop it into a lucrative "moon shine" business, because of the enormous public interest in what was going on.

One thing that surprised everybody in the SETI-NASA team was the moon people's unity, harmony and the governance of the entire moon population without a single leader. The absence of discriminatory divisions among their people the absence of political parties, absence of conflicts, absence of separatory boundaries - these were amazingly extraordinary features of their social system. No countries, nothing to kill or die for, no religions - as expressed in parts of the song "Imagine" by late John Lennon's came to their minds. "Imagine there's no heaven" seemed to be the only contrary part in the lyrics as the moon people believed in a heaven.

As time passed, Dooda and the others learned about the social structures of human societies on the earth and their history. Dooda was very surprised to learn of the enormity of divisions that prevailed among the people on earth. Though he could not understand the words describing race, religion, color, tribes, castes, countries, rich, poor etc., some of the pictures and video illustration he came across conveyed to him the feelings of division and discrimination that prevailed among earth people. Due to the sensitive nature of the moon people, these feelings were unfortunately being assimilated slowly into their brains. Dooda and Loola were the most exposed. Dooda being the pioneer in making contact possible with the earth people, he carried an extra feeling of responsibility to his elders and community. Dooda discussed these issues with his colleagues and elders. In spite of having a warm relationship with the earth people so far, the findings of these discriminatory divisions among earth people disturbed their psyches tremendously. When they learnt about various historical wars and killing of people, the moon people could not fathom at all how it was possible. They wondered whether the earth people were partly like carnivorous animals; when they finally found also that people on earth kill animals to eat their flesh as food, they were greatly horrified and deeply upset.

Though Seth and Max were very cautious in divulging sensitive and possibly offensive information to their moon friends, filtering out what were regarded as bad was a gigantic task. It was impossible to ensure that every piece of information that might be deemed sensitive to the moon people did not reach them as enormous quantities of data was exchanged between the two teams. Moreover assessment of what was sensitive to moon people was a judgmental issue. The significant expansion of team members at Seth's end over the past few months also added to the flow of un-scrutinized material to the moon people.

When the disturbing nature of information received from earth was discussed with the elders by Dooda on the first such occasion the elders cautioned Dooda and Loola. They were asked to ensure that any deficient behavior of the earth people that are not morally acceptable to the moon people should in no way be divulged to or discussed with the moon people. Dooda and Loola understood and agreed.

With time Seth and Max showed Dooda and Loola advanced technical devices and also achievements such as trains, aircraft, ships, hovercraft, rockets, international space stations, space shuttles, planetary explorations and even man's mission to the moon. The purpose was to get them to focus on the technical advancement and the inter-terrestrial missions capabilities of the earth scientists. Seth also thought that all these exchanges would give a hint to Dooda, about a possible future manned mission by Seth to see them personally.

When Dooda and Loola learnt that people from earth had already engaged missions to the moon, they were overwhelmed. Dooda jokingly asked Seth whether he was planning to visit him. Seth asked Dooda if he would like to have Seth as a visitor. Dooda replied yes! yes! yes! yes!. Seth said it could happen in the very near future. Dooda and Loola were thrilled.

Dooda and Loola thought of the enormous inputs that Seth could bring over to them if he were to journey over to the moon in a spacecraft. Of course their interest was in technical and educational inputs rather than gadgetry as their minds had not been corrupted by attachment to material excitement. Dooda's brain went into overdrive with the excitement that arose from this news and looked forward happily to the extra knowledge that he could gain. Loola's smile lit face indicated the same elation as was felt by Dooda. After watching the video clips of the previous moon missions they had no doubt that Seth's proposed visit would actually take place. After seeing the protective gear that the earth people had to wear when they landed on the moon, Dooda realized how harsh the environment on the outside moon surface could be though it was only just a few feet above their heads. For a moment he thought how lucky they were to be inside the caves. Dooda wondered how Seth would gain access into the cave as the moon people had never ventured into the alleyways found at a few restricted spots and which they believed to lead to the exterior or moon's surface.

Heaven ••• ••••

On an earlier occasion Dooda and Loola had learnt from Seth and Max the exact location of the earth in the solar system but they did not correlate this earth planet which was home to Seth and Max with the place in the sky that was known to them as heaven. However, when Dooda and Loola saw the pictures of the earth taken from the moon surface during the moon missions, they realized that their heaven was the same planet that Seth and Max referred to as their own world. The video clips they watched were more than adequate to clear any doubts on this. This puzzled them very greatly.

Though Dooda and Loola were extraordinarily intelligent scientists, they had been brainwashed from their childhood to believe that the beautiful object in the sky that they could see from certain locations of the moon's cave structure was the heaven where ultimately they would go to after death. Dooda has seen the heaven as a teenager during the short time he was traveling with the others. It was believed to be a very pleasant place full of pleasure and joy. Dooda's mind started scrolling

126

further "When our soul reaches there, we acquire beautiful youthful bodies ideally made for us to enjoy all the pleasures and joy available. How could this be wrong! Have I understood these things right? These psychological disturbances nagged and haunted both Dooda and Loola with relentless persistence. Dooda and Loola discussed with each other the conflicting evidence from the earth people on what was to them, their spiritual heaven. If Seth really lived in the heaven that they saw, then why was there so much discrimination, wars, killings, evil, and differences in that world, contradicting all we believed in argued Loola. Though Dooda was a scientist of high caliber now he had fallen into a state of severe psychological stress, worrying about what was going to happen to his soul after death. The only spiritual comfort he had enjoyed from a very early age had been permanently and irreparably shattered. The beautiful object in the sky that he had admired and gazed at so many times in his life had now undergone a drastic change and the idea that it was heaven was reduced to a mere myth. He could not reconcile himself to this new upside down situation nor could he find a source of comfort to help withstand the psychological disaster he experienced. Though the moon people had a system of beliefs that was almost totally lacking in dogmatism; yet the heaven concept was a strongly conditioned seed in their psyche. As they could see this heaven outside their world there was no doubt in their minds as to whether or not it existed. Their heaven was an object clearly visible to them from many parts of the moon unlike the heaven believed in by the people on earth who only conceived of it in their imagination.

At the usual video meeting on the next day, Seth and Max sensed keenly that Dooda and Loola were experiencing major emotional problems, but they could not figure out what it might have been. Seth did not get any clues from Dooda when he specifically inquired about it. "Have we done anything inappropriate to these extremely sensitive people?" Seth thought for a moment. Dooda and Loola requested Seth to playback the video clips showing the pictures of earth taken from the moon surface. Seth obliged without any hesitation or query. Dooda and Loola were watching the clips very intently. Seth thought Dooda and Loola were seeking to better understand details of Seth's intended visit. A few times when Seth tried to explain some aspect of the moon mission, the lack of interest shown by Dooda and Loola indicated that they preferred to watch the clip than listen to him. Dooda and Loola were also whispering to each other but their voice levels were too low for the microphone to discern the actual words spoken.

The video clips on the past moon missions more than confirmed that the same place that they regarded as heaven was the place that Seth and Max lived in. Dooda requested Seth to download the moon mission video to the portable camera as he wanted to show it to the elders. Seth asked Dooda as to why he was making this special request. Dooda was very truthful and explained what was going on in his mind. Dooda said that he had to inform the elders of his discovery and that the video would be helpful to convey the relevant information to them. Seth remembered that he was warned not to discuss belief aspects with the moon people by an advisory group in his team in the early days of the encounter. Notwithstanding the warning advice, Seth tried to explain some aspects of the belief system in his world. Dooda found them to be a heap of mythological concepts which had not brought any good to Seth's world as proved by the existing cruel and discriminatory nature of events in that world. "So, why is Seth trying to dump those ideologies on me? People on Heaven having different religions? Confusing!", thought Dooda. Following close on this thought was the next thought, "Seth is an intelligent man from a technologically advanced world but he did not talk intelligently on this subject, what could be wrong with him?" Dooda ended the session early, after saying "Bye! Bye!" to Seth. This was the worst session that they had ever had.

Elders' Verdict ••• ••••

After meeting the group of elders later on, Dooda and Loola explained to them the purpose of the meeting. On seeing Dooda's face the elders knew that he was in some sort of distress. Dooda either pretended that he did not hear the questions or genuinely did not grasp the questions that some of the elders raised. The elders already knew of the strong friendship that Dooda had with Seth and the mammoth knowledge base that was freely put at the disposal of Dooda by Seth and Max's group. Dooda informed the elders of Seth's planned visit to the moon. The elders were jubilant and wanted to know more details of when and how Seth proposed to make the journey. The elders could not understand the cause of the depression that Dooda and Loola were displaying. "Are they unhappy about Seth's intended visit? That cannot be" thought the elders.

Dooda was seeking to explain why he came to see the elders. He thought the information on the past manned missions to the moon would make the elders understand how Seth would come to visit them and also expected it to catch their attention as to what actually was Seth's world. When Dooda played back the moon mission video clips on the tiny portable camcorder screen all the elders congregated like a group of children to watch. They were utterly amazed by the vast technological advancements of the earth people and probably felt small too. All the news that the elders had been watching and receiving daily from earth was near magical and wholly alien to them. However, their innate level headedness kept them on in their normal life routines. When the elders saw the pictures of earth taken from the moon's surface they immediately knew what it was. It was the familiar picture of heaven that they had seen from several Cities many times over. Dooda explained to them that it was not any other but also Seth's world. All the people, animals, other objects and rituals and activities they had been seeing and watching all this time were from that world. The elders vehemently disagreed with Dooda. They explained that what they saw from various cities was heaven and it could not be the same as Seth's world. Elaborating further they said "People like Seth, though technically advanced, cannot be from heaven. Heaven is not a technically advanced material world. It is a beautiful natural world, with peace and serenity. From the moment you are there you enjoy everything. There is no sorrow, only happiness and you live forever. The people on Seth's world eat meat, they kill animals, they have wars and they are beings with divisive and discriminatory traits. So they could not be living in heaven. We warned you from the beginning not to show their socially unacceptable behavior to our people. They are not from heaven". Loola joined Dooda to jointly explain that the elders were totally mistaken. They played back the moon mission video clips a few times and each time pointed to different portions of evidence in support of their conclusions.

Finally the elders yielded and accepted Dooda and Loola's verdict and the entire gathering was plunged in a deeply reflective and painful moment of silence. The elders were very upset about the re-orientation that was becoming necessary to admit the new findings. Here was a moment that dealt a very destructive blow to their psyches. A revered idea that had existed over thousands of years without threat or challenge was shattered in a few seconds. More than half of those at the meeting including the elders were dumbfounded and motionless as if they had lost the power of speech and movement. The eldest of the elders broke the silence. He said "Well, this is a serious matter. We have been living in our world for thousands of years with our traditions, habits, unity, harmony, tolerance, peace, care and a trouble free and simple system that kept us content without any problems. All these years we did not have a method of comparing ourselves with any other beings elsewhere. We did not know or even imagine that there could be worlds outside our own, with life forms. But a few years ago, we accidentally encountered highly advanced beings from another world. We got much information of their life patterns from them. Some are very, very interesting while some others are brutal and even difficult to believe or understand. The time has come for us to open our eyes, learn from our observations and decide how we should fashion our path from here onward. I was shocked when I realized that the heaven that we believed in was not what we thought it was. It is somewhat the reverse of what we imagined, with a terrible history and practices of cruelty. This news will devastate our people, generating crippling psychological shocks on the whole community and result in irreversible damage to their minds. The social systems that helped us to exist in peace and harmony for millions of years will change drastically and could eventually cease to exist if we divulge this information to our brothers and sisters. As such we must now all promise each other not to divulge the new findings to anybody else. This is our duty as responsible citizens of the moon. After the twelve of us present here are dead and gone, none amongst the community will knows about this. I think this is the only way that we can contribute to our society to preserve our traditions and help prevent its destruction. I believe that this is the duty we are called upon to perform and it will be our biggest contribution to our community", he then fell silent. Everybody nodded their heads indicating their agreement. He started to talk again, "Dooda and Loola, we really appreciate the enormous work that you have done for our society. I know it is a very difficult thing for all of us, especially for you two, to agree to this. But we need to immediately terminate all connections that we have with the earth people and go back to the normal life routines that existed before these events of the recent past took place. I know you will all do it for our people. Please maintain complete silence on this matter and do not discuss anything or tell anyone why we had to do this".

Everybody looked at Dooda and Loola.

This was a shock for Dooda and Loola. Loola looked at Dooda thinking he might have something to say. Dooda tried to speak but no words came - he seemed to be about to have a mental breakdown.

Summoning a great deal of courage, Dooda asked the leading elder whether he could speak to Seth for one last time. He said he would explain all these things to Seth and request him not to seek to communicate with them or plan any mission to the moon to meet them in the future. The leading elder looked at the other elders. All nodded their heads to indicate their agreement to his suggestion. The leading elder requested Dooda to contact Seth as soon as possible and complete the task within a day or two.

As a final statement, the leading elder requested Dooda to take action to destroy the TV screen if Seth did not remove it from their vicinity. All these measures were discussed and arrived at in a very gracious manner. However, the tone of the leading elder's voice indicated the inherited authority and finality of a typical elder, evolved through thousands of years, within a proven successful and unbroken social system.

Dooda handed over the camcorder to Loola as he did not want to hold on to it anymore, symbolizing the near end of his link with the earth people. He then started walking back to the research station very feebly. Though Loola was following him, the emotional environment they were in did not warrant conversation. Halfway down, Loola separated from Dooda and headed towards the probe location. Dooda saw Loola going towards the probe but did not ask any questions. After having a last look at the camcorder Loola put it in the special slot it was meant to be placed in. The team on earth on duty at the time wanted to speak to him but Loola walked away at a faster pace than usual. The team wondered if this was a deliberate act. The team members on earth wondered what was going on with Loola, as they had never seen him behave in this manner before.

Dooda was a completely broken man now. He was not sure how he could convey the sad news to Seth and the group on earth and then make an abrupt termination of their warm and congenial relationship. The fact that he had to talk to Seth for the last time and thereafter cease all communications with the outside world was extremely traumatic for him. The emotional stress on his mind was more than he would be able to cope with. Neither Dooda or Loola could sleep in peace anymore, they were both thoroughly depressed.

As the issue of faith figured as a topic in their previous discussion, Seth and Max immediately sought advice from Shelton Dawkins who was an expert on human psychology. After absorbing the details of all that had happened, Shelton mentioned faith as a very emotional & delicate subject to deal with and blamed Seth for discussing it with the moon people. Shelton narrated the whole debacle as follows: "Assume that we people on earth see a four foot diameter moon like space object in the sky. This object is visually bigger than the moon and blue in color and shines like a gem. This object is millions of light years away from the earth, but due to its sheer size, it still looks large when viewed from earth. Say, due to the vast distance from us, it is impossible for the scientists on earth to get any information on this object other than to obtain an idea of the material that it is composed of, from a light spectrograph. Thousands of years ago when we became hunter gatherers someone introduced it as or claimed that this object was heaven. As nobody could prove or disprove this idea and this concept really helped to keep our mind and body in harmony the people on earth believed that this was in fact heaven. They already had a description of heaven which was that it was a place of happiness happier than any happiness one can feel experience or imagine. People were even ready to commit suicide to protect this idea. If a scientist denied this or someone even drew a cartoon ridiculing this idea the ardent believers would become very violent and militate against such affronts. Irrespective of all the strong arguments used against this idea, the idea will survive unless and until it is conclusively proven to be wrong. The large blue colored shining gem in the sky is our heaven and this idea symbolized by the object helped us over millions of years. When we are in trouble we go out, look at it and offer prayers seeking help from it. We get immense relief from our troubles at least psychologically every time we perform such rituals. Some practices involve animal sacrifice to obtain help from heaven to achieve favor. This builds up our faith in the object over our lifetime and we pass it on from generation to generation. People might perform paranormal acts or misinterpret natural events as miracles but somehow they attribute all these things to the blue big object in the sky as we believe in the idea which we have been brain washed to believe".

"Say one day quite unexpectedly a satellite which was sent by man 500 years ago managed to go past this object and sent pictures and other data to the earth. The pictures show that it is a barren object just like the planet Mercury and the surface temperature is thousands of degrees and the blue color is due to ionized gas. This is proof of the ordinary nature of the object. Then what happens to faith. What happens to the psyche of the man steeped in faith? What is the impact on society, the conglomeration of people who share a common belief? Heaven, hell, angels, ghosts among others are all entities rooted in the imagination. Our inclination and tendency to believe in these is inextricably linked to our psyche and plays a dominant role in our lives. The metaphysical or supernatural nature of these entities takes them out of the arena of proof and disproof and hence they continue to exist in the human imagination and to be debated till the end of time.

Belief and realization of truth are two facets. For example, say someone tells you that he has a gem enclosed in his fist. If we think what he says is true then the mental accord we constitute is "belief". The very moment he opens his palm and shows the gem the belief does not exist anymore and it turns into a state of "knowing". In fact that moment yields a state of realization of the truth. As such, there is a difference between belief and actual realization or experiencing. Mental streams that are associated with belief systems always have a certain degree of doubt attached, in keeping with this logic. Belief always dangles from a thread of doubt.

I believe this is exactly what happened to Dooda. He could not accept the actuality that he realized as he was a slave to his belief system. So

134

when you talk to him the next time, have this in mind. It will be a gigantic task for you to talk around it. I believe this is what caused him to get upset".

Shelton was dead right! How did he explain it so accurately?

Dooda and Loola reached the signal spot the next day at the usual time, meaning to talk to Seth's team for the last time. Only these two were there; presumably Loola instructed the others not to accompany them without offering any reasons. From the first word Hello! by Dooda; Seth, Max and the entire team who were at the earth station realized something had gone terribly wrong. With a lot of courage and a heavy heart, Dooda began.

"Dear Seth, Max and other friends... A few years ago when we received your LASER beam, we did not know what it was. We were fascinated by its glow; we touched it initially with fear thinking it might burn us. It did not, and then we played with it and enjoyed ourselves too. I blindly turned Loola's light beam to respond to your signal. I did not know that action would lead to an inter-terrestrial friendship. It is an unforgettable experience and the warmest friendship I have had in my lifetime. I will not be able to forget it however much I might try. I know you feel the same way. We were more than thrilled to learn that there were people beyond our world. We always thought people have to live inside the caves rather than on the surface until we saw your world. We were fascinated at how technically advanced your world was. Your group learnt our language in a very short time and was able to speak to us very fluently, making us comfortable to communicate with you freely. It gave us a feeling that we had been friends for thousands of years. You taught us a lot. We are very appreciative all what we learnt from you and we will remain indebted to you for forever. You gave us an exposure to your world that is still unimaginable to us. Every second that we were in touch with you, was an extremely happy and exciting moment. The pleasure we derived from those moments were even recollected in our dreams. And sometimes we felt we were in your world. When you said you will be visiting us, I was thrilled beyond words and I was looking forward to it."

Dooda was silent for a moment and was feeling uneasy. Loola passed on to him the container of water he had. Dooda sipped from it and continued his talk. Seth and the team knew he was preparing to say something unexpected and sad, but did not interrupt.

"You might wonder what I am trying to say. I will try to explain it briefly. Though we have been conversing with each other for some time, we really did not know exactly where you were from. I might have misunderstood it, and did not consider it seriously when I saw some of the pictures of your world taken from outer space earlier. However, when I saw the video recordings of your people landing on the outer surface of our world, we realized that you were from the exact same world as the beautiful gem like world visible to us from some of our cities. The people in the moon call this world the "Pleasure Place". In your language it is "Heaven". All of us in the moon believe that after our death we end up in heaven to enjoy an eternal life with nothing but joy and pleasure. Probably you may not be able to understand and I will not be able to explain how deep rooted this belief is among our people. With no disrespect to your world, when I realized my future dream world was not what I really imagined, I felt greatly tormented and took a long time to console myself. It was my duty to break this news to our elders. So, I summoned the group of elders in the city for a meeting. When I informed them about your intended visit, first they were very happy. After I showed your moon mission video to the group to show the possibility of your visit they were more than thrilled to understand it would soon become a reality. However, when I explained to them that you actually live in the world that we believe to be heaven, all the elders were upset and experience severe mental stress similar to the depression I had. You might not be able to understand the depth of that hopelessness and I will not be able to explain it in words either. We simply cannot divulge this to our fellow people. It will have an enormous impact on our social life that has been stable and flourished over the past thousands of years. All our people will be mental wrecks in no time. Look at me".

Dooda sobbed again, looked at Loola who turned his gaze away. More tears were flowing from Dooda's eyes than words leaving his mouth. Courageously he continued.

"I have got instructions to talk to you for the very last time and to end our relationship at the end of this message. As you know I am the person whose efforts resulted in contact with your world. I have a duty to perform to our fellow citizens for their protection, welfare and harmony. I need to respect our elders and carry out their instructions. This is the way our society works. I need to fall in line and respect the traditions we have practiced over thousands of years. As I have informed you we do not have written rules or a leader to report to; but this is how our system operates. The integrity of the system is more important to me than anything else. It is my duty to honor the system. With utmost reluctance I am compelled to make some requests off you, Seth. Seth, I trust that you will honor my request. Please, please, do not visit us. Make sure that nobody from your world will ever try to find us again, or send probes or any other investigative devices. Please, never send the LASER beam to us again. If any of these things happen then all that will be attributed to my irresponsible first action. Please understand me. After my last words please remove the screen, all other implements, retract the rod from the cave and take all the equipment up there to your world. This is my last conversation with you and after this I will never be coming back to this spot at all, ever. Finally I must say that I will never forget you and the others. Our friendship is so spacious like the enormous space between the two worlds. While I am feeling it so hard to say the final word goodbye to you, it tells me how lucky I am as I understand why I feel it so hard in me. For me this is worse than death. Though we are forced to depart, we are true friends forever. Our wounds will never heal but trust will become tools to be in touch with each other silently and closely. Rather than crying, if possible I will try to smile because it happened. The impression that you have left in our hearts will be there forever. I am truly sorry about this abrupt end to our journey as brothers. For the kindness you extended to us I am indebted to you. I wish you happy adventures, new friendships and peace for your world. I trust you will honor my request. Thank you."

After that he looked at Loola. Loola simply said "Thank you" and joined Dooda who was walking away from the scene. Seth and Max were stunned by all this but did not waste even a fraction of a second to respond. Seth said "Dooda, Dooda, please listen to me. I perfectly understand what your situation is, and what exactly you are requesting from us. But this should not be the way we should end our friendship. Can we talk? Can I talk to you tomorrow?"

Seth continued pleading with Dooda and Loola to stay back. He adjusted the probe's sound volume to the maximum presuming that he could catch their attention but it did not help. He was thoroughly disappointed. Dooda's talk was so emotional and intense, Seth could not think properly. Parts of what Dooda said kept reverberating in his mind making him more upset. It was the same emotional situation for all who were there with Seth. They could not imagine what impact this news would have on the entire population on earth which had also fused in as an integral though distinct and separate part of the whole interaction.

Seth and Max contacted all the counseling bodies they could access and called for an immediate meeting to discuss possible courses of action to be followed. After outlining the flow of events of the past few hours to all the participants, Seth inquired as to whether there was a way out to get his moon friends back to talk. The meeting had more silent moments than discussion periods. This was partly due to awaiting more people to join over the phone lines. Seth began to sort out his strategies and linked the meeting with many of his top notch collaborators from many

138

parts of the world who personally supported his work. Some were UN representatives who could influence many governments in the world. The meeting which was started with about 30 people initially, gathered more participants with the spread of the bad news, and finally had over 200 participants either physically at the meeting room or through other communication media. Whoever was requested to join did not think about how busy they were, time of day or any other factors that would otherwise have kept them out. Whole hearted prompt participation was seen due to the gravity of the situation. Abrupt termination of contact with the moon people was highly unacceptable to those who participated in the meeting or for that matter, for the entire world population, as the emptiness that would arise could not be taken lightly. Awaiting of news on the moon people and their interaction had become an ingrained part now of the lives of all people on earth after regular broadcasts had become the order of the day for the past two years. It would turn the entire world into a state of utter dejection and for how long the impact of the abrupt termination would last in peoples' minds was a difficult question to answer.

The participants did not feel the time passing as the discussion meandered into various topics and directions. Though it had already reached fourteen hours after it was started, nothing conclusive was forthcoming as a remedy. Most of the time was spent on assessing the grave situation that everyone expected would arise in the future, if the moon people held firmly to their decision not to ever talk to them again. NASA had to decide whether they should stop or go at a low pace on the work on the planned manned mission to the moon. Many dignitaries indicated that they could persuade their governments to comply with Dooda's request of not contacting them again if that was the eventual decision to be adopted. No one suggested aggressive or invasive action to reach the moon to find out more about the moon people and their social structures. However some religious leaders indicated that people on earth had a duty to educate the moon people about the "truth" though nobody had offered to explain unambiguous what that meant. Other than a suggestion to keep the observation activities to a minimum for a week or two and then review the situation at a later date, nothing concrete stood out as a feasible remedy at the end of the meeting. Seth and Max were not happy about the outcome of the meeting. Many times during the discussions Seth said he was obligated to Dooda to fulfill his request at any cost.

During the discussion some participants quoted references from scholarly articles published in accredited journals on this subject. According to those references, the scholars advocated complete non-interference by man to isolated human societies similar to the one found on the moon. The same policies were advocated even for small isolated human groups that have been remotely encountered in distant areas on the earth in places such as the Amazon wilderness. Such papers explained how modernized civilizations could influence and destroy in very short times, well established societies that had thrived over thousands of years. Seth and Max's brains were full of these ideas, suggestions and assurances given by participants. The meeting was adjourned after sixteen hours. After consulting Max, Seth directed all his team mates not to operate anything in the cave but keep their eyes and ears open on the instruments. By any chance if any one comes back to the vicinity of the camera, Seth wanted to be summoned immediately. With these instructions Seth ended his very long and disappointing day.

Loola went to see Dooda at his room on the following day, at their usual meeting time. Dooda was fast asleep. One of his colleagues told him that Dooda was not feeling well and went to sleep early. Loola hung around to talk to Dooda as he did not have anything to do. He too did not have proper sleep either. When Dooda got up Loola realized how weak Dooda was, and attributed the cause to the events just concluded. Though Loola said hello to Dooda, Dooda was silent and was constantly staring at the wall like a lifeless statue. Loola brewed a tea like drink and both shared it hot. After Dooda's cup was empty Loola re-filled both cups again. They did not converse but their body language suggested that they were sharing each other's sorrow and feelings. After about 40 minutes Loola indicated that he was leaving. Dooda made a gesture to him to wait for a while, and then he pulled out the very first poster he got from the probe, the only souvenir he had from Seth, and kept it on Loola's hand. Both looked at each other's eyes. Loola decided to take it with him. Respectfully, he bowed down, touched the right shoulder and left Dooda. Not a single word was spoken during all this time.

Seth and Max had been very disappointed for the last six days as nobody came to the vicinity of the probe. Other than a few birds that flew by and occasionally pecked at the camera to test the strength of their beaks, nothing was detected. Many times Seth thought that he would pull out all the equipment as Dooda requested and retire from his work. He had enormous support and encouragement from his fellow staff and influential people of reputed organization from very many countries, from the inception of the project. Some of these organizations provided very large sums of money and continued their generous financial assistance for the moon project. As such Seth was compelled to think broadly, not only to accommodate his aspirations but of others. He decided not to do anything foolish. But just like Dooda, Seth too was emotionally crushed after listening to Dooda's unexpected farewell speech.

Surprising everybody, on the seventh day the monitoring screen at the SETI-NASA center picked up an image of someone walking towards the probe. Seth and Max rushed to the station in double quick time. It was Loola. Seth increased the brightness of the light in the probe slightly so that they could see Loola clearly. Loola appeared very excited but sad. He looked at the screen which was at the usual position. He said "Seth and Max".

Seth jumped and said "Yes Loola, how are you. We are happy to see you. Are you OK?"

Loola said "Seth, I did not expect all these things to be here still after Dooda's request. After I saw this from afar and as we were very good friends I decided to come here and convey this news. I do not have much time. I have very sad news for you. Dooda is no more with us now. He was buried this morning. His health declined after he was here last. Please respect Dooda's last request and take back your equipment. He trusted you so much. Please, please, please". After saying these words Loola ran back in the direction he came from.

Seth immediately underwent a transformation. He became a different person as if possessed. He took control of the command center over all the satellites and the other equipment on the moon. As a first step he directed Collie to move towards a steep moon crater which was about three miles away from its present location. He set its speed to the maximum it could achieve and ensured that it was moving. Nobody interfered or questioned his actions. Next, he folded back the screen and retracted the telescopic rod into to master. He then carefully selected the coordinates of another crater. Max and the other staff realized that Seth was trying to eject "Master" and crash it into the crater. When their facial expressions indicating disapproval were noticed by Seth he took one single look at all of them that virtually made them freeze. Due to the sheer respect Seth earned during all these years no body wished to influence what he was trying to do.

On the pilot panel reserved for Collie's controls, the radar screen lights flashed to indicate it was heading beyond the controllable distance from Master. Though there were many audio and visual warning signs to stop its movement, Seth's attention was somewhere else. Nobody had the temerity to question Seth's actions. The sudden cessation of signals coming from Collie indicated that it would have tumbled down into the crater. As an expert space vehicle commander, Seth relayed commands to "Master" to rise from the ground. He then maneuvered Master towards the crater that he selected and made it turn around and crash into the center of the crater. Finally he commanded all the satellites to

142

fly out of their orbits and crash on the near side of the moon. It was now obvious to everyone that the project was over. They were concerned as to what stress or trauma would now befall Seth.

Seth cried like a baby and mumbled to Max that he was happy that he fulfilled Dooda's request. The atmosphere at the center was quite the opposite of what it was on the day that they spoke to Dooda and Loola for the very first time. It did not take much time for the news to reach all corners of the world. People had mixed reactions on Seth's actions.

Seth summoned a meeting with all those who joined him at the last meeting as he had to make a statement.

Many of Seth's friends spoke to him personally over the phone commending his action but some blamed him for having been hasty. The invitees to this emergency meeting did not give as much ready attention as at the previous occasion. After nearly fifty companions arrived for the meeting he commenced explaining the reasons behind his actions.

He said "As human beings we should respect each other more than anything. Now I could visualize the damage we were doing to the moon people's society with more and more of our influence and interference. Dooda's speech was an eye opener to me in the matter of respecting each other's belief systems on which human societies are built. Everybody should realize the amount of influence that a belief system can have on the structure of a human society. Belief systems influence the architecture of our buildings, the food we eat, legal systems we follow, our customs, rituals we observe and how we behave".

He continued, "When I was very young I dreamt of being able to communicate with an alien in my life time. I did exactly that. I am happy and sad about the can of worms that I opened. I will not be engaged in this line of work in the future and urge everybody to respect Dooda and honor his request. I am leaving this message to all my global friends in many countries to influence their governments to honor Dooda's request. All human beings with a conscience should do that. I am to be blamed if anyone starts looking for moon people again. I thank all who supported me in various ways to accomplish my dream".

Just as Seth was about to finish his farewell speech with the announcing of his retirement, he was passed a small note from his partner and friend Max.

The note read: Twenty five minutes ago a secret CIA Bulletin was issued on detection of a rocket launch from earth; Evidence so far, strongly points to it being a mission to the moon launched from a location in the Asian region. Separate evidence has also emerged of a strong worldwide interest in prospecting for "Babaloniums". Speculation is rife that this might be one of the primary goals of the mission............."

"Oh, shit!" exclaimed Seth, banging his head on the desk.

•••• ••• •• •

"There is enough for everybody's need,

but not enough for anybody's greed"

Mahatma Gandhi